Cody stared at the little girl standing on the porch.

He couldn't catch his breath. He stared into a tiny heart-shaped face he'd never seen before, and yet seemed so familiar. The little girl had Bailey's straight blond hair and rosebud mouth. His gaze stopped at her eyes. It was there that he discovered the truth.

Six years traveling, riding bulls, and it came down to this. To a child with stormy blue eyes wearing jean shorts, a T-shirt and pink cowboy boots.

He had a daughter.

"I tried to tell you." Bailey looked away, the breeze blowing her hair around her face.

"You didn't try very hard."

"The day you left I told you that I loved you and that we needed to talk. You laughed and walked away because 'cowgirls always think they're in love.'"

Cody remembered that day. He remembered thinking if he didn't get away, he would drown in her. At twenty-five, he'd been too afraid of love to take a chance. He'd been too afraid of failure.

Now he had a daughter.

Books by Brenda Minton

Love Inspired

Trusting Him
His Little Cowgirl

BRENDA MINTON

started creating stories to entertain herself during hour-long rides on the school bus. In high school she wrote romance novels to entertain her friends. The dream grew and so did her aspirations to become an author. She started with notebooks, handwritten manuscripts and characters that refused to go away until their stories were told. Eventually she put away the pen and paper and got down to business with the computer. The journey took a few years, with some encouragement and rejection along the way—as well as a lot of stubbornness on her part. In 2006, her dream to write for Steeple Hill Love Inspired came true.

Brenda lives in the rural Ozarks with her husband, three kids, and an abundance of cats and dogs. She enjoys a chaotic life that she wouldn't trade for anything—except, on occasion, a beach house in Texas. You can stop by and visit her (not at the beach house) at her Web site, www.brendaminton.net.

His Little Cowgirl
Brenda Minton

Steeple
Hill®

Published by Steeple Hill Books™

STEEPLE HILL BOOKS

Steeple
Hill®

ISBN-13: 978-0-373-87502-3
ISBN-10:   0-373-87502-9

HIS LITTLE COWGIRL

And ye be kind one to another, tenderhearted,
forgiving one another, even as God for Christ's
sake hath forgiven you.

—Ephesians 4:32

This book is dedicated to:

Doug, for always supporting me in my dreams, and to my kids for allowing me to be the "crazy mom." Dream big and never give up.

To all of my family and friends who have kept me going forward when I wanted to quit.

To Janet Benrey and Melissa Endlich, for everything they do and have done for me.

To Janet McCoy of McCoy Ranches, for taking the time to answer my questions about bull riders and bull riding. (Mistakes I've made are of course my own.) To bull riders like Cord McCoy, who are an inspiration and a role model to young people, and who leave their own footprints of faith.

To the readers for reading.

To God for all of the blessings.

Chapter One

Bailey stuck her hands into the hot, soapy water and began to scrub the dishes she'd put off washing until after lunch, wishing for the umpteenth time that the dishwasher still worked. Her father had helped for a few minutes, until his legs had grown weak and he'd taken himself to the living room and his favorite recliner to watch *Oprah*.

The throaty snore she heard through the doorway told her that he'd fallen asleep. She didn't mind; it was sleep that he needed these days. At least when he was sleeping, he wasn't worrying.

Oprah's voice drifted into the kitchen, borne on the gentle breeze that blew through the house. "So tell me, Suzanne, how much did you pay for your home in Malibu?"

Bailey strained to listen. "Three million, a bargain." Audience laughter.

Bailey shook her head and scrubbed harder. Three million for a house. What couldn't she do with three million dollars? She looked out her window above the sink, at the farm shimmering in the late-afternoon sun. It looked as tired as her dad. A good eye could see that things were falling apart. The fences were sagging and the last windstorm had done a number on the barn roof. Not to mention her truck, which was on its last leg, and tires.... Three million dollars. That would help pay the mortgage. Well, of course, with three million dollars in the bank, there wouldn't be a mortgage.

She was doing well if she made the mortgage payment each month. The tips she earned as a waitress put shoes on her daughter's feet—one pair at a time—and cutting a few more cows from the herd would pay the property taxes. Life in the Ozarks was far removed from Hollywood.

A little cutting back, a lot of prayer and making it through another day with her dad still in her life. That was how it went in the real world. At least in her world.

Bailey squeezed her eyes shut. She opened them when she heard a distant rattle and the rapid-fire bark of her blue heeler. Her mind turned, wondering who it could be. She wasn't expecting anyone, and it sounded like whoever it was, they were pulling a trailer.

She squeezed the water out of the dishrag, tossed it on the counter and walked out the back door. If she didn't catch the dog now, the person paying them a surprise visit would have a hole in his pant's leg and a bad attitude to go with it. Bailey was holding on to faith by a string; she didn't need someone's bad day to rub off on her.

A shiny, red extended-cab truck pulling an RV rumbled to a stop. Blue, her five-year-old blue heeler, stood in the middle of the yard. The yard that really needed to be mowed before it became a hayfield.

But Bailey stopped herself there and reached for the dog's collar. She had a list of things that needed to be done. All of those things dimmed in comparison with the bigger problem she saw stepping out of the truck and into her life.

The hair on the back of Blue's neck was standing on end. Teeth bared, the dog strained against her hold on his collar. For a brief, really brief, moment, she considered letting go.

Six years had passed since she'd seen Cody Jacobs face-to-face. Six years since she'd spent a summer working on a ranch in Wyoming. Six years since she'd tried so hard to tell him she was pregnant. Six years since she'd given up because he wouldn't answer her phone calls.

Now he was here. Now, when there were so many other worries to work through. She looked up to see if God would send her a sign, a parting of the clouds or some other gigantic miracle. Instead she felt a soft whisper of peace. If only it hadn't gotten tangled with dread and a good dose of anger as her day went suddenly south.

Cody walked across the lawn, looking for all the world like he belonged on her farm. He was suntanned, wore faded Wranglers, and a soft, cotton T-shirt stretched across his broad shoulders. He was smiling like he hadn't a care in the world.

Every time she had imagined this moment, she'd thought what she'd say. She'd be strong, send him packing, show him she was in control and that he couldn't hurt her again.

Not once had she been breathless or speechless. Not once in her imagination had she thought that she'd remember how his laughter sounded on a quiet summer night in Wyoming, or how his hand had felt on hers. She had told herself that she'd only remember him saying goodbye and how he laughed when she told him she loved him.

All of her imaginings melted like a snowman in July when faced with the genuine article—Cody Jacobs walking toward her. Now what in the world was she going to do about that? What was she going to do about the little girl inside the house, and the truth that she'd kept from him? All of her good intentions—wanting to protect her daughter from someone whose lifestyle had seemed unfit for a child—seemed irrelevant at the moment.

Cody Jacobs was about to learn he had a daughter. She hadn't wanted it to happen like this. Meg knew who her daddy was. Bailey had wanted to confront Cody in her own way, when the time seemed right.

Not today.

Blue yanked at the collar and jerked her forward a few feet, a warning that her visitor had entered the imaginary danger zone of the dog. Bailey flexed her fingers and wished she wasn't leaning forward the way she was.

"Bailey, you're looking good."

Her foot she was looking good. She was wearing the same faded jeans and stained T-shirt she'd worn while working in the garden.

"Thanks, Cody."

Still smiling, he held his hand out to Blue. The dog suddenly forgot that the man was the enemy. Pulling free from her grasp, the animal belly crawled to Cody. Bailey stood, stretching the kink from her back. Her gaze connected with Cody's, really connected for the first time since he'd gotten out of the truck.

Up close and in person he was still about the prettiest man she'd ever seen. Like the average bull rider, he wasn't tall, just a few inches taller than her five feet five inches. He still had lean, boyish looks and long eyelashes that could make a girl swoon—if she were the swooning type. Bailey wasn't, not anymore.

"How've you been?" He closed the gap between them, his hand still being licked by Blue.

"I'm fine." Most days she really was. "What are you doing in Missouri?"

She knew the answer. She was a convenient stop on the highway to Springfield, just thirty miles north. The town was hosting a pro bull-riding event, and Cody was in line for the world title this year.

"I wanted to talk to you."

"Okay, talk."

Looking suddenly unsure, he took off his bent-out-of-shape, straw cowboy hat and shoved his fingers through black hair, which was straight and a little too long. When he looked at her, with his stormy blue-gray eyes, she thought of Meg and how she didn't want Cody to learn the truth without any warning.

Her heart shuddered at the thought. With a quick glance over her shoulder, she breathed a sigh of relief. Meg was taking a nap on the couch. That gave Bailey a few minutes to decide the best course of action.

"Bailey, I'm here to say I'm sorry." Cody shrugged and said, "I guess this is part of a man turned thirty and realizing he's wasted a lot of years and hurt a lot of people."

"I'm not sure what to say." The words of his apology were much as she had imagined them to be, but in her dreams they made more sense. In real life his words didn't bring instant healing.

"You don't really have to say anything. This is something I have to do. I…" He cleared his throat and brought his gaze up to meet hers. "I joined AA and part of the process is making amends for the things I've done. I know that when I drove away from Bar A Ranch, I hurt you."

"So is this about wanting forgiveness, or are you truly sorry?"

She needed more than words because words were easy enough to say. Words promised forever and something special on a summer night.

Words said *I'm sorry* and even *I forgive*.

Cody worried the hat in his hands, keeping his head down and his gaze on his dusty boots. When he looked up, his eyes were clear, his jaw set and determined. She had seen that look on his face before, normally with a camera focused in tightly as he gave the nod and the bull he was set to ride busted from the gate for an eight-second ride that always seemed to last eight minutes.

"This is about me needing forgiveness, and it is also about being truly sorry."

It was her turn to look up, to search for something in his gaze, in those eyes that reminded her of a summer storm on the horizon. He meant it, or at least she thought he did. She nodded and took a step back.

"Okay, you're forgiven."

"You mean it?"

Did she mean it? She closed her eyes, wanting him to be gone, wanting to walk back into the house to a sink full of dishes and chores waiting to be done. Those were the things that made sense to her these days.

What also made sense was Meg, and the life they had here, the life they had built for themselves in spite of everything. Bailey had paced the floor alone when her daughter had been colicky. Bailey, alone, had held Meg tightly when a bad dream woke her in the middle of the night.

Cody hadn't been there, not even for that stormy night when Bailey's dad had driven her to the hospital.

Her conscience poked at her, telling her that he couldn't apologize for the things he didn't know. Cody couldn't apologize for leaving her to raise a child alone, not when he'd never known about that child. They'd both made mistakes. He didn't know it, but they both had apologies to make.

"I forgave you a long time ago." She smiled, feeling the heat of the August sun on her head and back.

"That means a lot to me, Bailey. I want a fresh start, and I didn't want to make that start thinking about you and what happened."

What happened—the way he said it made it sound simple and easy to forget. It wasn't easy to forget a decision that made a person feel like she'd let down not only herself, but everyone who counted on her. Even God.

Maybe Cody was finally starting to understand.

"That's good, Cody. I hope that this is the change you need." She paused, unsure of how to proceed. She should tell him about Meg. Before he left she should let him know what she had tried to tell him the last time she saw him.

The screen door thudded softly behind her. Bailey lifted her gaze to his, fearing the truth and the look on Cody's face. He stared past her, his eyes narrowing against the bright sunshine. As his gaze lingered, Bailey knew that the time for truth had arrived.

It had never happened this way in her dreams.

"Mommy."

Cody stared at the little girl standing on the porch. He tried to catch his breath, but the weight on his chest pushed down, forcing air from his lungs as his heart hammered against his ribs. He stared into a tiny heart-shaped face he'd never seen before, and yet, and yet, the face seemed so familiar.

The little girl had Bailey's straight blond hair. She had a rosebud mouth, just like her mom's. His gaze stopped at her eyes. It was there that he discovered the truth and he knew that Bailey had apologies of her own to give.

Six years of traveling, riding bulls and putting money in the bank for a place of his own, a place he wouldn't let his own dad buy for him, and it came down to this. It came down to a child with stormy-blue eyes wearing jean shorts, a T-shirt and pink cowboy boots.

Cody felt a huge dose of regret because while he'd been having the time of his life, Bailey had been here raising his daughter alone.

With a million questions and plenty of accusations racing through his mind, he switched his attention back to Bailey. She twisted away from him but not quickly enough for him to miss the streak of red creeping up her neck.

Cowgirls couldn't lie.

"Go inside, Meg," Bailey said.

"But I need a drink."

"Get a juice box out of the fridge. I'll be in soon."

"Who is he?" The little girl crossed her tanned arms and gave him the look that said she was the only law in town and he was trespassing. He wanted to smile but he couldn't. Not yet.

"He's someone I used to know."

The little girl nodded and walked back into the house, the screen door slamming behind her. Bailey waited until her daughter, his daughter, too, was out of sight before facing him.

"It looks like I'm not the only one who needs to apologize," he whispered, not really sure if he could say the words aloud.

He had a daughter. He was six months sober, living in an RV, and he had a daughter.

He was on step 9, and it seemed that Bailey had a Step 9 of her own. Making amends.

"I tried to tell you." She looked away, the breeze blowing her hair around her face. He remembered the feel of her hair, like soft silk and feathers.

He remembered that being with her had made him believe in himself. For a few short months he had believed he could be something better than his own father had been. Now he couldn't find that feeling, not with anger boiling to the surface.

"You didn't try very hard."

"The day you left the ranch, I told you that I loved you and that we needed to talk. You laughed and walked away because, and I quote, *'Cowgirls always think they're in love.'*"

As she faced him with his own stupid actions, it was his turn to look away. He focused on the same tree-covered hill her gaze had shot to moments ago. Without really trying, he remembered that day. He remembered getting in his truck and driving away, with her running out of the barn trying to stop him.

He remembered thinking that if he didn't get away, he would drown in her. More memories returned, along with the knowledge that he had wanted to lose himself in that feeling. That had scared him more than anything. At twenty-five he'd been too afraid of love to take a chance. He'd been afraid of failure.

Now he had a daughter. He was in the middle of a program that included not starting new relationships, and this one had to be taken care of. He had a little girl. He needed to wrap his mind around that fact and what it meant, not just for the moment but for the rest of his life.

"I should have listened to you." He ran his hand through his hair and shoved his hat back in place. "But you could have told me. You've had six years of opportunities to tell me."

"I left messages for you to call me. After a while I gave up. Wouldn't you?" She crossed her arms, staring him down with brown eyes that at one time were warmer than cocoa on a winter day. "You were running so fast, Cody. You didn't want to hear what I had to tell you because you were afraid it would be about love and forever."

"You should have told me."

"And have you believing that I was trying to trap you? The day you left Wyoming you made it pretty clear to me that you weren't looking for 'forever' with anyone."

He needed to sit down. He didn't want to think about how much he needed a drink. Six months sober, and he wasn't going to end his sobriety like this.

"Bailey, don't throw my words back in my face. That was six years ago. I've learned a lot, and I've been through a lot." He shook his head and took a step back from her.

"Keep your voice down."

"And on top of that you want me to be calm about this?"

"I'm sorry."

He remembered her at twenty-two. She had dreamed of being a famous horse trainer with a ranch and a few kids. He'd been running from those kinds of women, the kind who dreamed of forever.

"I won't keep you from seeing her." She made it sound like the offer of the century.

"Of course."

"In case you're wondering, she knows that you're her dad. I haven't kept that from her. But you're not on her birth certificate."

"Did you ever stop to think that maybe she needed to see me?"

"When would she have seen you? Maybe once or twice a year as you drove on through? Or on TV with a pretty girl on your arm."

"Is that how you portrayed me to her?"

She sighed and shook her head.

Of course she wouldn't do that. He knew that much about her. Bailey was kind. She had faith, and he'd taken advantage of her innocence. That had haunted him for years. Her tears had haunted him, too, and her regret.

"I told her that someday she could meet you."

"That's great, Bailey." He took a step back. "I have a daughter and you were going to let me meet her *someday*?"

"What did you expect from me, Cody?"

"Bailey, I don't know the right answer to that. I just know that I have a daughter and she's five years old. Don't ask me to make sense of this or tell you how I would have reacted a few years ago. I'm a different person today."

"Older and wiser?"

"Something like that."

He couldn't adjust with Bailey staring at him with soft brown eyes and a guilty flush staining her cheeks. He had to get away from her because he didn't know if he should hug her or throttle her.

"I need to think."

She shrugged as if it didn't matter. But he could tell that it did. It mattered to him, too.

And he had honestly thought he'd be able to stop by, say his apologies and leave. He'd been surprised on more counts than one. He'd been surprised with a daughter, and surprised that Bailey Cross still had the ability to undo him.

"I have to ride in Springfield tonight." He walked to his truck, followed by the tongue-wagging blue heeler. He turned when he realized that Bailey was right behind him. "I'm leaving my RV here so that you'll know I'm coming back. I'm not a twenty-five-year-old kid now, Bailey. I don't run."

"I'm sure you don't."

"Maybe I shouldn't even go to Springfield."

"I think you should go, Cody. You can call and we'll talk this out." She took a few steps toward him, and he hadn't counted on the rush of feelings and memories that returned. "I know you can't miss this ride. I know you're at the top of the point standings."

"Bailey, some things are more important than eight seconds on a bull. Family is more important."

"I know that. But I also know what this world title means to you."

"I'm coming back," Cody said. "Tonight."

He leaned to unhitch the RV from the back of his truck, aware that she stood next to him, her hands shoved into the front pockets of her jeans.

"Fine, you can come back and we'll talk." Bailey backed up a step, as if wanting that distance between them. "We'll work something out."

"Work something out?" He shoved the tongue of the trailer off the hitch and turned to face her. "You make it sound like we're disputing over a property line and not a little girl with eyes like mine."

"Cody, I am sorry."

He shook his head and raised his hand to wave off her words. Instead of staying to argue, he got into his truck and pulled away. When he glanced into his rearview mirror she was walking across the lawn to the farmhouse where she'd grown up.

And inside that house was a little girl he should have known about, a little girl who needed to know her daddy. He wasn't going to walk away this time. Bailey Cross would have to find a way to deal with that.

Bailey stopped on the back porch, lingering for a long moment in the breeze created by the overhead ceiling fan. Inside the house her dad and daughter were waiting.

Driving down the road was the man who had given her that child and broken her heart. Her head was spinning like the blades on the ceiling fan.

She'd forgiven him. She had really thought she'd forgotten. Instead it all returned in a heady flash of memory, including remnants of the pain she'd felt when he'd left her in Wyoming.

After Meg's birth she had done what she'd been taught— she'd pulled herself up by her bootstraps and moved on. As a single mother coping with lonely nights and an uncertain future, she hadn't had time for wallowing in her mistakes.

How was she going to deal with Cody Jacobs? Worse, how was she going to deal with the fact that having him back in her life had turned her emotions inside out?

And then came fear. Would he take Meg away from her? Would his knowing about their daughter mean that holidays and summer vacations would be spent apart? How would she cope with sharing Meg?

Bailey stopped the downward spiral of thoughts. She wouldn't be sharing Meg with a stranger. Cody was Meg's dad. He had rights.

That assurance didn't make her feel any better.

She leaned against the side of the house, waiting for the world to right itself before crossing the threshold to face her dad. The dog lumbered up the steps and belly crawled across the porch. Bailey reached down and Blue nuzzled her hand as if the dog knew she needed to be comforted.

"Thanks, girl."

When she walked into the kitchen, her dad was there, waiting for her. Bailey pulled a pitcher of tea out of the fridge and pretended that nothing had happened. Not that she'd get away with pretending. Her dad had probably heard the entire conversation through the open window.

"Who were you talking to?" Jerry Cross was leaning on the counter, his afternoon meds in his hand. His skin had lost the healthy farmer's tan he'd always worn. Now he just looked old and gray. And he wasn't old.

Every time Bailey looked at him and saw him wasting away in front of her, she wanted to cry. She wanted to explain to God that it wasn't fair. She had lost her mom when she was ten. Now she was losing her dad.

And Cody Jacobs's RV was parked in her driveway.

"It was…" She turned to see if her daughter was in the room.

"She's watching that goofy cartoon she likes."

"That was Cody Jacobs."

"Humph."

"He came to apologize."

"I guess he got more than he bargained for." He coughed, the moment of breathlessness lasting longer than a week ago and leaving him weak enough that he had to sit at the kitchen table. "His RV is still here."

"He says he's coming back."

Her dad looked almost pleased. "Good for him."

"Good for him? Dad, this isn't good for me. It isn't good for Meg."

"Maybe it's good for me." He wiped a large, work-worn hand across his face. "Maybe I need this, Bailey. Maybe I need to know that he's here for you."

"He showed up to apologize. That doesn't put him in my life. I don't want him in my life. I don't want to be his girl of the week. Isn't that what the announcers on the sports channel call the women who hang on to his arm?"

"We've both noticed a change in him since that bull trampled him last winter." Once broad shoulders shrugged. "People change."

Bailey couldn't agree more. She had changed. At twenty-two she had gone to Wyoming for a summer work program, starry-eyed and thinking that all cowboys were heroes. She had come home four months later, pregnant and brokenhearted.

It had taken her more than a year to forgive herself and move on. She had struggled with the truth, that God's grace was sufficient. She had grown and learned how to stand on her own two feet without dreams of a man rescuing her.

Now she had a dad and a little girl who needed her. She had a farm with a second mortgage, back taxes seriously in arrears and medical bills piling up in a basket on the coffee table. She had horses that needed to be fed.

"Dad, I have to get to work. You have to let me be an adult and take care of this myself."

Moisture shimmered in her dad's brown eyes. "I know you can take care of things, Bailey. I only wish I could help you more."

She hugged him tightly, her heart breaking because of his continued weight loss.

"Don't worry, Dad. We have peace, remember?"

"Peace." He nodded as he whispered the word.

Bailey walked to the back door. "I need to walk to the back pasture to check on that cow that didn't come up this afternoon. Can you keep an eye on Meg?"

"I'll watch her." He swallowed his pills before continuing. "He has a right to know his daughter."

"I know."

She knew, but she didn't quite know how to deal with it, not yet. Cody now knew about Meg. It had to happen sooner or later. She wouldn't have been able to remain out of the rodeo circuit forever. Avoiding Cody had meant avoiding people who could send horses her way for training.

Maybe God had meant for it to happen this way, with Cody driving into her life when she had the least amount of energy to fight? And maybe, just maybe, he would meet Meg and then leave town.

Chapter Two

Bulls bellowed and snorted, the sound combining with the steady hum of the crowd and the banter of cowboys, medical staff and stock contractors. Cody leaned against the wall in a corner of the area that was almost quiet.

"What's up with you?"

"Bradshaw, I didn't know you were here." Cody smiled at the guy who had been a friend for years. Rivalry had come between them a few times. And for a while Jason Bradshaw's faith had driven a huge wedge between them.

Cody hadn't known what to do when his friend "found religion" two years earlier. They had gone from being drinking buddies to strangers, both wanting different things out of life.

The rift had grown until the day seven months earlier when Cody had woken up in a hospital, unsure of who he was or where he was. Later he had watched tapes of the fall. The wreck of the season, they called it. He had been twisted in the bull rope, dangling from the side of a fifteen-hundred-pound animal. When Cody came loose, the bull twisted and the two butted heads with a force that had given him a huge concussion and some loss of memory.

Jason said it must have knocked some sense into him, because the Sunday after his release from the hospital Cody gave in to the urge to attend the church service the bull riders held each week. He had stood next to his friend, hearing a message his grandfather had tried to tell him when he had been too young to understand. Later on in life he had thought he didn't need it.

That Sunday he knew he needed it. He knew that he needed to be forgiven. He needed the promise contained in those words, and he needed a fresh start.

He had never dreamed his second chance would lead him to Gibson, Missouri, and a little girl named Meg.

"You look like you got hit by a semitruck." Jason nudged Cody's side, gaining his attention.

"Something like that."

"Did you see Bailey?"

Cody moved to the side to see why the crowd was roaring. He watched a young rider make it to eight seconds and then some. The kids on tour were going great guns with enthusiasm and bodies that weren't being kept mobile with cortisone injections, Ace bandages and a diet of ibuprofen.

"Remember what that felt like?" Jason laughed and watched as the kid on the bull jumped off, landing on his feet and running out of the arena without a limp.

"Vaguely." He remembered what yesterday felt like, when he knew who he was and that his life was all about winning the bull-riding championship and walking away with a seven-figure check. Now his goals were as scrambled as his insides.

"I found out today that I'm a dad. I have a five-year-old daughter named Meg."

Jason took off his hat and ran a hand through short red hair, his eyes widening as he leaned back against the wall. His being speechless didn't happen often. Cody was sort of glad his friend reacted with stunned silence. His surprise validated Cody's own feelings of disbelief.

"Wow."

"Is that all you have to say?"

Jason laughed and shrugged his shoulders. "Congratulations?"

"Thanks. I think."

"What are you going to do?"

"Well, if Bailey was seventeen and madly in love with me, I'd do the right thing and marry her. Right now she's about twenty-eight, and I'm pretty sure she hates me. So that leaves the little girl. I might have a chance with her, but I'm not sure."

His daughter, a sprite with her mother's perky nose, heart-shaped face and flaxen hair. Cowgirls were hard to beat. They were tough as nails and soft as down. Until you made them mad. Bailey was definitely mad. She had a right to be, but that didn't help Cody.

He had a daughter. It was still sinking in. Thinking back, he remembered the luminous look in Bailey's eyes when she said she loved him, and then the tears when he teased her about cowgirls always thinking they were in love. Finally there were the frantic phone calls that lasted five or six months after she left Wyoming. It all made sense now.

He looked down, shaking his head at the tumble of thoughts rolling through his mind. He had missed out on five years. Without knowing it, he had become his own dad.

"Cody, don't beat yourself up for something you didn't know about."

"If I had called her back, I would have known. Instead I

went on my merry way, thinking she just wanted to cry and try to drag me back into her life." He fastened the Kevlar vest that bull riders wore for protection and tried to concentrate on the ride about to take place. "I should have known Bailey better than to think that about her."

"You know, I think you only ran because you were so stinking in love with her." Jason laughed as he said the words, his loud outburst drawing the quick glances of a dozen men in the area.

"Do you think you could announce it to the whole world?"

"Sorry, but I think they're going to find out sooner or later."

Cody pulled off his hat and ran shaking fingers through his hair. "I could use a…"

"Friend to pray with?" Jason smiled as he replaced the word with something that wouldn't undo six months of sobriety.

"Yes, prayer." His new way of dealing with stress. "I have a daughter, Jason. What in the world am I going to do with her?"

"Buy her a pony?"

"My dad bought me a pony."

Jason slapped him on the back. "Go back to Gibson, Missouri, and get to know your daughter. You've got enough money in the bank to last more than a few years, and a good herd of cattle down in Oklahoma. Maybe it's time to start using your nest egg to build a nest? You could even use that business degree of yours for something other than balancing a feed bill and tallying your earnings."

"What if I can't be a dad?" He didn't know how to be something he'd never had. That's why he'd run from girls looking for "forever."

"No one really knows how. I think you just learn as you go. It's probably a lot like bull riding, the more you work at it, the better you get."

Someone shouted Cody's name. He was up soon. He tipped his hat to Jason and told him he probably would lay off the tour after this event, at least for a few weeks, at least until he settled things with Bailey.

And he would give up ever being a world champion. His goal and his dream for more years than he could remember had been within his grasp, but one afternoon in Gibson, Missouri, had changed everything.

Five minutes later he was slipping onto the back of a bull named Outta Control. He hated that bull. It was part Mexican fighting bull and part insane. As he pulled his bull rope tight, wrapping it around his gloved hand, the bull jerked and snorted. The crazy animal obviously thought the eight seconds started before the gate opened.

Cody squeezed his knees against the animal's heaving sides and hunched forward, preparing for the moment that the gate would open. Foam and slobber slung around his face as the bull bellowed and shook his mammoth head.

"This is crazy." He muttered the words to no one in particular as he nodded his head and the gate flew open.

If he survived this ride, he was going back to Gibson, to his daughter and to Bailey. He would find a way to be a dad.

The fact that Cody's RV was still in the drive the next morning meant nothing to Bailey. The problem was, his truck was there to. That meant he'd survived his ride and returned.

She didn't know how to feel about Cody Jacobs keeping promises. Six years ago they'd been sitting around a campfire when he leaned over and whispered that he loved her. She had believed him. She had really thought they might have forever.

She wouldn't be so quick to believe, not this time. This time she would protect her heart, and she would protect her daughter.

Changed or not, Cody was a bull rider, and the lure of the world title would drag him back to the circuit, probably sooner than later.

"He got in at around midnight. He was walking straight but a little stooped." Her dad had followed her to the porch. He pressed a cup of coffee into her hand.

"What were you doing up?"

"Praying, thinking and waiting to see if he'd come back." Jerry Cross smiled.

"Nice, Dad. It sort of makes me feel like you're plotting against me."

"Not at all, cupcake." He scooted past her and back to the kitchen. "Want me to feed this morning?"

"Nope, I'll do it. I have to face him sooner or later." She glanced over the rim of her cup and watched the dark RV. "You mind listening for Meg?"

"Honey, you know I don't. And you know I don't mind feeding."

"It's too hot. The humidity would…" Her heart ached with a word that used to be so easy.

"Don't cry on me, pumpkin. And the humidity isn't going to kill me." He winked before he walked away.

Bailey prayed again, the silent prayer that had become constant. *Please God, don't take my dad.* She knew what the doctors said, and she knew with her own eyes that he was failing fast. She didn't know what she'd do without him in her life.

She drained her cup of coffee and walked out the back door. The RV in the drive was still dark and silent. The barn wasn't. As she walked through the door, she heard music on the office radio and noises from the corral.

Cody turned and smiled when she walked out the open

double doors on the far side of the barn. Her favorite mare was standing next to him, and he was running his hand over the animal's bulging side.

That mare and the foal growing inside of her were the future hope of Bailey's training and breeding program. If that little baby had half the class and durability of his daddy, the Rocking C would have a chance of surviving.

"Any day now." Cody spoke softly, either to her or to the mare. She and the mare both knew that it would be any day.

"What are you doing here?"

He glanced up, his hat shading his eyes. "I told you I'd be back. I'm in it for the long haul, Bailey."

"In what for the long haul?"

He shot her a disgusted look and sighed. "I'm a father. I might be coming into this a little late, but I want to be a part of Meg's life."

"So, you've gone from the guy who didn't want to be tied down to the guy who is in fatherhood for the long haul?"

"When confronted with his mistakes, a guy can make a lot of changes." He slid his hand down the mare's misty-gray neck, but his gaze connected with Bailey's. "I'm alive, and God gave me a second chance. I don't take that lightly."

"I see." But she didn't, not really.

Bailey walked back into the barn, knowing he followed. When she turned, she noticed that he wasn't following at a very fast pace. The limp and slightly stooped posture said a lot.

"Take a fall last night?"

He grinned and shrugged muscular shoulders. "Not so much of a fall as a brush-off. This is what one might call 'cowboy, meet gate—gate, meet cowboy.' The bull did the introductions."

"Anything broken?" Not that she cared.

"Just bruised."

"Good, then you should be able to hitch that RV back to your truck and leave today."

"Actually, no, I can't. Funny, I've never really had a reason to stick before, but I like Missouri and so this isn't such a bad thing. And the folks at the Hash-It-Out Diner all think you're real pretty and a good catch."

Bailey searched for something to throw at him, just about anything would work. She wanted to wipe that smug smile off his face. Especially when smug was accompanied by a wink and a dimpled smile.

"Cody, I don't need this. You don't understand what it's like here and how long it took me to rebuild my reputation after that summer in Wyoming."

He didn't understand about going to church six months pregnant, knowing God forgave, but people weren't as likely to let go of her mistake.

"I didn't tell them who I am, or that I'm Meg's dad." He turned on the water hose as he spoke. "I think most of them have gotten over it, Bailey. Except maybe Hazel. Hazel has a daughter in Springfield who is a schoolteacher and a real good girl."

Bailey groaned as she scooped out feed and emptied it into a bucket. Cody dragged the hose to the water trough just outside the back door. He left it and walked back inside.

"Yes, Maria is a good girl. I'll introduce the two of you." She managed a smile.

"Bailey, I was teasing." Smelling like soap and coffee, he walked next to her. "This isn't about us, or a relationship. This is about a child I didn't know that I had. I'm not proposing marriage, and I'm not trying to move in. I want the chance to know my daughter."

Bailey glanced in his direction before walking off with the bucket of grain and the scoop. She remembered that he had shown up for a purpose other than his daughter.

"Why did you come to apologize?"

"It's a long story."

"I have thirty minutes before I need to leave for work."

Cody took the bucket from her hand and started the job of dumping feed into the stalls. "You water, I'll feed. And they told me you work three days a week at the Hash-It-Out."

"Since Dad can't work, we do what we can to make ends meet." She didn't tell him that the ends rarely met. "So, about you and this big apology."

"Why can't your dad work?"

"He has cancer."

She couldn't tell him that her dad had only months to live. Saying it made it too real. And she couldn't make eye contact with Cody, not when she knew that his eyes would be soft with compassion.

"I'm sorry, Bailey."

"We're surviving."

"It can't be easy."

Cody poured the last scoop of grain into the feed bucket of a horse she'd been working with for a few weeks.

"It isn't easy." She turned the water off and then finally looked at him. "But we're doing our best."

"Of course you are." He sat down on an upturned bucket, absently rubbing his knee as he stared up at the wood plank ceiling overhead.

"Let's talk about you, Cody. What happened?"

"Bailey, I'm an alcoholic. I started AA about seven months ago. I've been sober for six months." He shrugged. "About five months ago I wrote out a list of people I had hurt, people that I needed to apologize to. You were at the top of the list."

"I see. And how did this all start?"

"Apologizing, or realizing that I needed to grow up and make changes in my life?"

He smiled a crooked, one-sided smile that exposed a dimple in his left cheek. Bailey hadn't forgotten that grin. She saw it every time Meg smiled at her. It reminded her of how it had felt to be special to someone like him. He had picked her wildflowers and taken her swimming in mountain lakes.

That moment in the sun had happened when her dad had been healthy and the farm had been prosperous. Their horses had been selling all across the country, and they'd had a good herd of Angus. Now she had five cows, two mares, no stallion and a few horses to train.

"What made you go to AA?"

"I turned thirty and realized I didn't have a home and that I had a lot of blank spots in my memory. I was getting on bulls drunk." He shrugged and half laughed. "I realized when I got trampled into the dirt back in Houston last winter."

"I saw you on TV the night it happened." She closed her eyes as the admission slipped out and then quickly covered her tracks. "I've always watched bull riding. Dad and I watch it together."

"Gotcha." He leaned back against the wall. "I guess one of the big reasons for changing was that I didn't want to waste the rest of my life."

"I'm glad you're doing better." It was all she could give him. She was glad he was sober and glad he was safe. "We'll work something out so that you can get to know Meg."

"Get to know her? Bailey, she's my daughter and I want more than moments to 'get to know her.' I want to be a part of her life."

"You can, when you're in the area."

"I made a decision last night." He didn't smile as he said the words. "I'm not leaving."

"What does that mean?"

"It means I'm staying in Gibson, Missouri."

Bailey's heart pounded hard and she shoved her trembling hands into the front pockets of her jeans. Dust danced on beams of sun that shot through the open doors of the barn, and country music filtered from the office. She had been here so many times and yet never like this, never as unsure as she was at that moment.

"What about the tour? You're closer than ever to winning a world title."

She knew what that meant to him. She knew how hard it was for bull riders to walk away from the pursuit of that title.

"Some things are more important. And if I choose to go back, bull riding will always be there."

"You can't stay here."

"I'm going to park my RV under that big oak tree by your garage, and I am most certainly going to stay."

"This is my home, my property, and I beg to differ."

"And that's my little girl you've got in that house, so I think you'll get over it."

Bailey sat down on the bucket he'd vacated, her legs weak and trembling. She looked up, making eye contact with a man she didn't really know. He wasn't the guy she'd met in Wyoming, the one who'd said he didn't plan on ever having a family or being tied down to anyone. Back then she had thought finding the right woman to love would change him. Now she didn't want him changed and living on her farm.

She had to get control. "Fine you can stay for a week, and then we'll work something out."

"I'm not leaving, not until I decide to go."

"Cody, I don't have time to argue with you."

He shrugged, casually, but obviously determined. His mouth remained in a straight line, not smiling and not revealing that good-natured dimple.

"I've lost five years of my daughter's life, Bailey. I'm not losing another day. Don't take this personally, because I'm not trying to make it personal, but I'm not letting you call the shots. You're not going to keep my daughter from me."

Did it look that way to him? She hadn't meant for that to happen. She had really thought he didn't care, or wouldn't care. He was in this life for a good time. Those had been his words the day he walked away from her.

People did change. He wasn't the only one who needed to apologize.

"I'm sorry. I never meant to keep her from you." She glanced down at her watch and groaned. "I have to go to work."

"I'll be here when you get home."

Would he? She didn't know how to deal with that thought. Of him in her life, and in her daughter's life.

She had learned to rely on God and the knowledge that He would get her through whatever came her way. If she closed her eyes, she could think of a long list of *whatevers*. At the top of the list was losing her dad; then came being a single mom, and then the pile of bills that were growing as large as Mount Rushmore. God could get her through those things.

Now she had to worry about Cody and what his staying would mean. Would he try to gain custody of Meg, or visitation? Would he stay only long enough to prove that he had rights?

How would it feel if he walked away? She tried to tell herself that she wouldn't be hurt. This time it would be different because now the person who would be hurt was Meg.

Bailey wouldn't let that happen.

Chapter Three

Cody stood outside the barn and watched Bailey drive away, the old truck stirring up a cloud of dust as it sped down the rutted gravel drive. When he turned toward his RV, Jerry Cross was there. It had to happen sooner or later, that the father of the woman he'd gotten pregnant would want to take a piece out of his hide.

If someone ever hurt Meg that way, Cody would like to think he'd be there to do the same thing. It would help to start off on the right foot. "Hello, sir. I'm Cody Jacobs." Father of your grandchild.

"Are you staying?" Jerry sat down in the lawn chair that Cody had unfolded and stuck under the awning of the RV.

"Planning on it." Cody grabbed another chair out of the back of his truck and plopped it down next to Jerry's.

"Think she'll let you stay?"

"The way I see it, she doesn't really have a choice."

Jerry laughed at that, the sound low and rasping. Cody glanced sideways, noticing the tinge of gray in Jerry's complexion. It couldn't be easy for Bailey, having her dad this sick and handling things on her own. The condition of the farm pretty much said it all. The barn needed repairs, the fence was sagging and the feed room was running on empty.

"I like you, Cody, and I hope you'll stick around. Let me give you some advice, though. Bailey isn't a kid anymore. She isn't going to be fooled. She's strong and she's independent. She takes care of this farm and she juggles the bills like a circus clown." Jerry's eyes misted over. "I worry that life is passing her by and she isn't squeezing any joy out of it for herself."

"I didn't mean to do that to her."

The older man shrugged shoulders that had once been broad. Cody couldn't imagine being in his shoes, knowing that life wouldn't last and that people he loved would be left behind.

"It wasn't all you, son. I have more than a little to do with the weight on her shoulders."

"Is there a way I can help?"

Jerry shook his head. "Nope. Others have offered. She's determined to paddle this sinking ship to shore. She thinks she can plug the holes and make it sail again."

"I've got money…"

Jerry's gnarled hand went up. "Save your breath and save your money. She won't take charity."

"It isn't charity. I'm the father of the little girl in that house."

"Then I guess you'd really better tread lightly."

Jerry stood, swaying lightly and balancing himself with the arm of the chair. Cody reached but withdrew his hand short of making contact. If it were him, would he want others reaching to hold him up, or would he want to be strong on his own? He thought that Jerry Cross wouldn't want a hand unless it was asked for.

That made him a lot like his daughter.

"I'm going in to check on the young'un. Holler if you need anything," Jerry said as he walked away.

The young'un. Cody sat in the chair and thought about the little girl. His daughter. For a long time he waited, thinking she might come out of the house. When she didn't, he went to the barn.

Thirty minutes and two clean stalls later, a tiny voice called his name. Cody swiped his arm across his brow and peered over the top of the stall he had been cleaning. Meg stood on tiptoes peeking up at him. He hid a grin because she was still wearing her nightgown and yet she'd pulled on those pink cowboy boots she'd been wearing the previous day.

"I have kittens." She chewed on gum and smiled.

"How many?"

"Four. Wanna see 'em?"

He wanted to see those kittens more than anything in the world. A myriad of emotions washed over him with that realization. He had never hugged his child. He hadn't held her or comforted her. He hadn't wiped away her tears when she cried. Five years he had missed out on loving this little girl with Bailey's sweet face and his blue eyes.

"I do wanna see 'em."

He opened the stall door and joined the little girl that barely reached his waist. Her hand came up, the gesture obvious. Cody's heart leaped into his throat as his fingers closed around hers.

In that instant he knew he'd follow her anywhere. He'd give his life for her. And if anyone ever did to her what he'd done to her mother…

Regret twisted his stomach into knots. He couldn't undo what he'd done to Bailey, but he could do something now. He could be a father. Or at least make his best attempt.

Doubt swirled with regret, making him wonder if he could. What if he couldn't? What if he turned out to be his own father?

"The kittens are in there." Meg pointed to a small corner of the barn where buckets and tools were stored. The area was dark and dusty, but a corner had been cleared out and straw put down for the new mother.

"How old are they?"

"One week. They don't even have their eyes yet."

Cody smiled and refrained from correcting her about the eyes. "I bet they love you."

She shook her head. "Not yet, 'cause I can't touch them or the momma kitten will hide them. She's afraid they'll get hurt."

"Momma cats are like that." He peeked into the corner and saw the mother cat and the four little ones.

"There's a yellow tabby, a gray, one black cat and a calico. I like calico cats best."

"I think I do, too." Little fingers held tightly to his, and at the same time it felt like they were wrapping around his heart.

Meg led him from the area. "We can't stay long or she'll be mad."

"We wouldn't want to make the momma mad."

"My mom is mad at you."

Cody had never been fond of amusement-park rides. He could handle eight seconds on the back of a bull, but that up-and-down roller-coaster feeling was one he couldn't hack. And this felt like a roller coaster.

"I'm sorry that she's mad at me, Meg. Sometimes adults need time to work things out."

He kneeled in front of his daughter. Her mouth worked her gum as she stared into his eyes. When she rested her hand on his cheek and nodded, his eyes burned and he had to blink away the film of moisture.

"I know you're my daddy." She nodded at that information. "My mom told me about your eyes when I was just a little kid."

"Meg Cross, you're about the sweetest girl in the world." And he hoped he wouldn't let her down.

As he was thinking of all the mistakes he could make, his daughter stepped close and wrapped her arms around his neck. Her head rested on his shoulder and he hugged her back.

He wouldn't let her down. He wouldn't let her grow up thinking that a dad was just the guy who sent the check each month. Whether he stayed in Gibson, or settled somewhere else, he would be a part of his daughter's life.

The alarmed bark of Blue ripped into the moment. Cody hurried from the barn with Meg holding tightly to his hand. He scanned the yard, past his RV to the house. He saw the dog near the back porch and next to him on the ground was the still form of Jerry Cross.

Bailey didn't feel like working. She felt like going home and being by herself. Not that she could be alone at home. And today would be worse because Cody would be there, wanting to talk.

Why in the world did he suddenly think they needed to talk things out? Had he been watching afternoon talk shows and learning about sharing feelings?

Or was it just a step in a program?

She sighed, knowing she wasn't being fair and that God wanted her to give Cody a chance because grace was about being forgiven. She knew all about grace.

"Why do you look like someone messed with your oatmeal?" asked Lacey Gould, her black hair streaked with red, as she walked up behind Bailey, who was starting a fresh pot of coffee. The two of them had been unlikely friends for four years. They didn't have secrets.

Lacey didn't know who Meg's dad was. That was something

only God and Bailey's dad knew. That was Bailey's only secret from her friend.

"I don't even like oatmeal." Bailey poured herself a cup of coffee and reached for the salt shakers that needed to be refilled.

The Hash-It-Out had been busy nonstop for over an hour. Now the crowds had waned down to the regular group of farmers who gathered for mid-morning coffee and good-natured gossip.

Lacey grabbed the pepper shakers and started filling them. "Rumor has it someone showed up yesterday driving a new truck and pulling an RV. And another rumor states that the truck and RV are still in town."

"Rumor has it that the rumor mill in this town could grind enough wheat to feed a small country."

"Cute. That doesn't really make sense, but it is a little bit funny." Lacey pulled ten dollars from her pocket and slid it across the counter top. "You had a four-top leave this the day before yesterday."

Bailey knew better. She didn't reach for the money. Lacey had a bad habit of trying to help by lying. She was a new Christian and her heart was as big as Texas, even if she didn't always go about helping the right way.

"You keep it."

"It's yours."

Bailey shook her head. "Good try, sweetie, but I didn't have a four-top the other day."

Lacey shoved the money into the front pocket of Bailey's jeans. "Stop being a hero and let a friend help."

The phone rang. Bailey glanced toward the hostess station and watched Jill answer. The older woman nodded and then shot a worried glance in Bailey's direction, with her hand motioning for Bailey to join her.

"I'll be right back." Bailey touched Lacey's arm as she walked toward the hostess.

"Honey, that was someone named Cody, and he said he's taking your daddy to the hospital in Springfield."

The floor fell out from under her. Lacey was suddenly there, her hand on Bailey's. "Let me get someone to drive you."

"I can drive myself."

"No, you can't."

Bailey was already reaching for her purse. She managed a smile for the two women. "I can drive myself. Could you let Jolynn know that I had to leave?"

"Sure thing, sweetie, but are you sure you're okay to drive yourself?"

Bailey nodded as she walked away from Jill's question. At that moment she wasn't sure about much of anything.

In a daze she walked out the door and across the parking lot, barely noticing the heat and just registering that someone shouted hello. Numb, she felt so numb, and so cold.

It took her a few tries to get the truck started. She pumped the gas, praying hard that the stupid thing wouldn't let her down, not now. As the engine roared to life she whispered a quiet thank-you.

Springfield was a good thirty-minute drive, and of course she got behind every slow car on the road and always in a no-passing zone. Her heart raced and her hands were shaking. What if she didn't make it on time? What if this was the end? She couldn't think about losing her dad, not yet, not now when she needed him so much.

"What if he's gone and I don't get to say goodbye?" She whispered into the silent cab of the truck, blinking away the sting of tears.

She couldn't think of her dad not being in her life. He had

always been there for her. He had been the one holding her hand when her mother died, and the one who drove her to the hospital when Meg was born.

Her dad had been the one who hadn't condemned her for her mistake. He had loved her and shown mercy. He had insisted that everyone makes mistakes. Without those mistakes, why would a person need grace?

Those who are healthy aren't in need of a physician. In those months after she had returned from Wyoming, she had really come to understand the words Jesus had spoken and the wonderful healing of forgiveness.

Her dad had taught her to bait a hook, and to train a horse. He had taught her how to have faith, and to smile even when smiling wasn't easy.

"Please, God, don't take him from me now."

Roots, this all felt very much like putting down roots. Cody's mind swirled as he waited for Bailey to arrive.

In the last few years he hadn't stayed in one place longer than a month. He usually spent time between events parked at the farm of a friend where he kept his livestock.

With Bailey's dad sick and Meg in his arms, thoughts of leaving fled. He had never known how to stick. Now he didn't know how he could ever think of leaving.

He knew himself well enough to know that before long the lure of bull riding would tug on him. Between now and then he would pray, hoping that when the time came he would make the right choices.

He knew enough to know that there wouldn't be any easy answers.

The door of the ER swished open, bringing a gust of warm air from the outside. Cody shifted the sleeping child in his lap and turned. Bailey stood on the threshold of the door, keeping it from closing. She watched him with a look of careful calculation, her gaze drifting from his face to her daughter.

Their daughter.

He couldn't stand up to greet her, not with Meg curled like one of her kittens, snuggling against his chest. She felt good there, and he didn't want to let go.

Cody didn't want to hurt Bailey. It seemed a little too late for that. Her brown eyes shimmered with unshed tears, and if he could have held them both, he would have.

Bailey crossed to where he was sitting. She looked young, and alone. She looked more vulnerable than the twenty-two-year-old young woman he'd known in Wyoming.

"Is he…"

"He's alive." He answered the question she didn't have the heart to ask. "He had an episode with his breathing. They're running tests. That's all they'll tell me because I'm not family."

Bailey sat down next to him. "I don't know what I'll do without him."

"He isn't gone, Bailey."

She only nodded. Shifting, he pulled a hand free and reached to cover her arm. With a sigh she looked up, nodding as if she knew that he wanted to comfort her. Her lips were drawn in and her eyes melting with tears. The weight of the world was on her shoulders.

He wanted to take that weight from her. He wanted to ease the burden. He wanted to hold her. He moved his arm, circling her shoulders and drawing her close, ignoring the way she resisted, and then feeling when she chose to accept. Her shoulder moved and she leaned against him, crumbling into his side.

"I won't leave you alone." He whispered the words, unsure if she heard but feeling good about the promise.

Time to cowboy up, Cody. He could almost hear his grandfather say the words to a little boy who had fallen off his pony.

The door across from them opened. A doctor walked into the room, made a quick scan of the area and headed in their direction. He didn't look like a man about to give the worst news a family could hear. Cody breathed a sigh of relief.

"Ms. Cross, I'm Dr. Ashford. Your dad is resting now. We've given him something to help him sleep and moved him to the second floor. You should be able to take him home in a day or two." He reached for a chair and pulled it close to them. "I'm not going to lie—this isn't going to be an easy time, and it might be better if you let us send him to a skilled-care facility."

"I want him at home. He belongs at home." Her stubborn chin went up and Cody shot the doctor a warning look.

"The family always wants that, but you have to consider yourself. How are you going to take care of him? You work, you go to town, and he's there alone."

Bailey's eyes closed and she nodded. Her face paled and Cody knew what she was thinking. She was blaming herself for not being there when her dad collapsed. She was thinking of all the ways she'd let him down.

"Bailey, you aren't to blame for today. I was there. I shouldn't have left him alone."

"He isn't your responsibility—he's mine." She moved out of the circle of his arm. "I should have been there for him."

The doctor cleared his throat. "Neither of you are to blame. Ms. Cross, your father has cancer. He isn't going to get better. He's going to get worse. You have to accept that you aren't going to be able to give him the twenty-four-hour-a-day care that he needs."

"But I want him home now, while he can be at home."

"You have to think about…"

"He's my responsibility," Bailey insisted, cutting off the

doctor's objections. This time her tone was firm enough to stir Meg.

"Bailey, you have two choices." Cody got her attention with that, and she glanced up at him. "You can either let me help or you can put your dad in a facility where he can be watched over while you're at work."

She shifted her gaze away, focusing on the windows that framed a hot August day and afternoon traffic. "I know. I just didn't want it to be this way. I wanted him to get better."

"He can't, Bailey, not on this earth. I know that isn't what you want to hear, but sometimes the way God heals is by bringing a person home to Him, to a new body and a new life."

Shock and then relief flooded her expression as tears pooled in her eyes and then started to flow. Cody shifted Meg and reached to pull Bailey back into his arms.

Her head tucked under his chin and her body racked with grief, he held her close and let her cry. He wondered if she had cried at all before then, or if she had been so busy taking care of everyone else that she hadn't allowed herself to grieve.

He glanced up, making eye contact with the doctor, who was looking at his watch and starting to move. Bailey's sobs quieted and she leaned against his side. Meg had awoken and was touching her mother's face, her sweet little hands stroking Bailey's cheek.

How had he gotten himself into this? Last week he had been a guy with a new faith in God and in himself, trying to make changes and making amends. And now he was here, holding Bailey and knowing he couldn't leave.

Adjusting to the wild buck of a bull was easy compared with this. A bull went one direction, and a countermove on his part put him back in control, back in center. No such luck with this situation.

On a bull they would have called the situation, "getting pulled down in the well."

"Bailey, I won't let you go through this alone."

She moved from his embrace, as if his words were the catalyst she had needed to regain her strength. The strong Bailey was back, wiping away her tears with the back of her hand.

"I appreciate your offer to help, Cody. I really do, but I know that you have a life and places you have to be."

He shook his head at what she probably considered was a very logical statement. To him it meant that she still didn't expect him to stay. And it probably meant that she didn't want him in her life.

"Bailey, we'll talk about the future, but for now I'm staying and I'm going to help you with your dad and with the farm."

He meant it, and she would have to learn that his word was good.

Chapter Four

Bailey looked out of the kitchen window and breathed in the cool morning breeze. She used to love lazy summer mornings, the kind that promised a warm day and not too much humidity. Two years ago she would have spent the morning doing chores and then packed a picnic to take to the lake.

This was a new day. Her dad was home from the hospital, but the doctor was certain they wouldn't have him for long. How did a person process that information?

By going on with life, as if nothing was wrong? Bailey was trying. She was making breakfast, thinking about work on her to-do list and planning for Meg's first day of school in two weeks.

School—that meant letting go of her little girl, and it meant school supplies and new clothes. In the middle of all of the *normal life* thoughts was the reality. Her dad was in bed, and Cody was living in an RV outside her back door.

How could she pretend life was normal?

Eggs sizzled in the pan on the stove, and the aroma of fresh coffee drifted through the room, mixing with the sweet smell of a freshly mown lawn. Bailey glanced out the window again, eyeing the mower still sitting next to the shed, and then her gaze shifted to the man who had done the mowing. He walked out of the barn, his hat pushed back to expose a suntanned face.

It should have felt good, seeing the work he'd done in the two days since her dad had come home from the hospital. Eggs frying and coffee brewing should have been normal things, signaling a normal morning on a working farm. Instead these were signs of her weakening attempts at keeping things under control. Make breakfast, do the laundry, dust the furniture, which would only get dusty again, the little things that signified life was still moving forward.

She reached into the cabinet for a plate and slid the eggs out of the skillet. A light rap on the back door and her back instinctively stiffened.

"It's open."

The screen door creaked and booted footsteps clicked on the linoleum. And then he was there, next to her, pouring himself a cup of coffee. Had she actually dreamed of this, wanted this to be her life—Cody in her kitchen, pouring a cup of coffee, sitting across from her eating breakfast?

If so, the dream had faded. Now she dreamed of other things, of making it, and of a stable full of other people's horses to be trained, and money in the bank. Romance was the last thing on her mind, especially when she hadn't even brushed her teeth this morning and her hair was in a scraggly ponytail.

It didn't help that he smelled good, like soap and leather. Maybe romance wasn't the last thing on her mind. This opened the door for other thoughts, the kind she quickly brushed away, reminders of his hand on her cheek and the way it had felt to be in his arms.

"Are you going to work today?" He turned and leaned against the counter, his legs crossed at the ankles and the cup of coffee lifted to his lips.

"I can't work." She answered his question as she flipped a couple of eggs and a few slices of bacon on the plate with already buttered toast.

"Can't work? Why?"

"Because my dad needs me here. I can't leave him alone with Meg." She handed him the plate.

Cody set his plate down on the counter. He turned to face her, his jaw muscle working. Bailey shifted her gaze from the storm brewing in his blue eyes. She picked up the dishrag and wiped crumbs from the toaster off the counter. A strong, tanned hand covered hers, stopping her efforts to distract herself. She slid her hand out from under his and looked up.

"I'm here, Bailey. I'm trying to help you."

"Why, why are you here now?"

"I want to be here." He sipped his coffee and then set the cup on the counter. "I know I can't stay forever, but I'm here and I want to help."

How many people had tried to help and had accepted her refusal, and her insistence that she could do it herself? How long had she been holding on to the reins, telling herself she could do it all, while everyone called her stubborn? It wasn't stubbornness; it was determination, and maybe a survival instinct she hadn't recognized until recently.

It was a mantra of sorts. Keep going, keep moving forward, don't slow down or you might not make it. She had become a horse with blinders, able to only focus on the job at hand. She didn't want to lose focus.

"I ordered supplies to fix that north fence." His carelessly tossed-out words jerked her back to the present.

"I didn't ask you to do that. I can't afford it right now."

"I'm paying for the materials."

"Cody, you have a career. You can't let go of your place

standing." She let her gaze drift away from his. "And really, I don't expect you to foot the bill around here."

He mumbled under his breath and walked away from her.

"What about your breakfast?" she called out after his retreating back, noticing the dark perspiration triangle between his shoulders. He'd been up for a while, working.

"I don't think that cooking my breakfast is your problem." He turned at the door. "Bailey, you push me further than any woman ever has. On so many levels. Get in there and get ready for work. If you don't, I'll load you up and drive you myself."

And then he was gone. The sound of his retreating footsteps sent a shudder up her spine. When she glanced out the window, she saw him walk into his camper, the door banging shut behind him.

"Sis, you're going to have to let someone help—it might as well be Cody."

Bailey turned, fixing her gaze on her dad. He had hold of the back of a kitchen chair, his knuckles white with the effort. She turned back to the normal thing, fixing breakfast and pretending her dad would be around for another twenty years.

"I know, Dad. I know that I need help, we need help, but I don't know…"

"How to accept help." The chair scraped on the linoleum as he sat at the kitchen table, pushing aside yesterday's paper and a pile of mail. "You learned that stubbornness from me. Now let me teach you something new: Let someone help you out. It'll make the burden that much lighter."

He paused for a long time. Bailey turned with his plate and a cup of coffee. His head was buried in his hands, and his shoulders were slumped forward. Bailey put the plate down on the table and touched his arm. His hand, no longer steady, came up to rest on hers.

"Sis, it would make my burden lighter if you'd let him help."

And that was the way he shifted it, from her to him, no longer her problem. She knew he had planned it that way. He knew that she'd do it for him when she couldn't do it for herself. She leaned and kissed the top of his head.

"For you, Dad." But it wouldn't be easy, not when the long-forgotten memories of a Wyoming summer were starting to resurface, reminding her of what dreams of forever had felt like.

The light rap on the thin metal door of the RV announced her arrival. He had seen Bailey crossing the yard, her mouth moving as she talked to herself, more than likely about him and the unpleasant things she'd like to do or say.

He opened the door and motioned her in. She stood firm on the first step and didn't accept his offer. The hair that had been held in a ponytail was now free, blowing around her face, and the slightest hint of pink gloss shimmered on her lips.

"I'm going to work."

"Okay." He knew it couldn't be easy for her, letting go of pride and having him be the one who stepped in to help.

She shoved her hands into the front pockets of her jeans. "I need to show you his medication and how to give him the injections. Can you handle that?"

"Bailey, you know that I can." He'd given more shots than a lot of veterinarians. Growing up on a ranch, he'd doctored his own livestock. There hadn't always been a vet on duty, or one that could get to them fast enough.

"You'll have to make lunch. I won't be home until after two."

"I know that."

"Meg will need a nap."

"I can handle it."

She chewed on her bottom lip, her brown eyes luminous as she stared up at him. He reminded himself that he was here because he had a daughter, not because he meant to become a part of Bailey's life.

Other than that summer in Wyoming, he'd never really been a part of any woman's life. He hadn't allowed himself those forever kinds of entanglements. He wasn't about to find out he really was his father's son. But then, hadn't he already found that out? He had walked out on Bailey, and he hadn't been there for Meg.

Neither of his parents had really taught him about being there for a person, or about sticking in someone's life.

"Let me turn off my coffee pot and I'll be right over."

Bailey nodded and then she walked away. He watched her cross the lawn to the house, her shoulders too stiff and her head too high. He wondered if she was really that strong or if she was trying to convince herself. He thought the latter was probably the case.

Switching off the coffee pot and then the lights over the small kitchen, he walked out the door of the RV, ignoring the jangle of his cell phone. The ring tone was personalized and he knew that the caller was one of his corporate sponsors. They wanted to know when he'd be back on tour. He didn't have an answer.

Unfortunately he had their money and he had signed a contract. That meant he had certain obligations to fulfill. He needed to be seen, on tour, on television and wearing the logos of the corporations on his clothing.

There weren't any easy answers, and there was a whole lot of temptation trying to drag him back into a lifestyle he'd given up months ago. He wasn't about to go there. He was going on seven months of sobriety, and with God's help, he planned on making his sobriety last a lifetime.

When he walked into the house a few minutes later, Bailey was sitting at the kitchen table with a plastic container full of pills and individually wrapped needles.

"You don't have to worry, Bailey, I can do this."

She nodded, but she didn't have words. When was the last time she had really smiled, or even laughed? He sat down across from her, pushing aside those thoughts.

"Show me what to do."

She did. Her hands trembled as she explained about the pain meds and the pills. She explained that Meg wasn't allowed to drink soda, and that she should have milk with her lunch.

He felt as if he should be taking notes. Shots, cattle and fixing fences were easy; being this involved in someone's life was a whole new rodeo. He wasn't about to ask what five-year-old girls ate for lunch.

"I have to go. What I just showed you, I also wrote on that tablet." She nodded toward the legal pad on the table and stood, immediately shoving her hands into her front pockets. "If you have any problems…"

"We won't."

"If you do, call me. I can be home in ten minutes." She headed for the door. "Oh, if you get any calls about horses, I put an ad in the Springfield paper for training. My rates are in the ad, and no, I can't come down in price."

He followed her to the door. "I'll take messages."

"Cody, I appreciate this."

He shrugged, as if it didn't matter. "I'm here as long as you need me."

He waved as she got into the truck, and he tried to tell himself this would be easy. Staying would be easy. Helping would be easy. Rolling through his mind with the thoughts of staying were the other things he didn't want to think about, such as his place at the top of the bull-riding standings, his obligation to his sponsors and the herd of cattle he was building in Oklahoma.

Bailey parked behind the Hash-It-Out Diner, the only diner, café or restaurant in Gibson, Missouri. No one seemed to mind that the tiny town nestled in the Ozarks had a shortage of businesses. They had a grocery store and a restaurant; of course they had a feed store.

And they had churches. In a town with fewer than three hundred people, they had four churches—and every one of them was full on Sunday. So the town obviously had an abundance of faith.

If the people in Gibson needed more than their small town had to offer, they drove to Springfield. Simple as that. And on the upside, since Gibson didn't have a lot to offer, it didn't draw a lot of newcomers.

What Bailey loved was the sense of community and the love the people had for one another. Gossip might come easily to a small town, where people didn't have a lot to do, but so did generous hearts.

Not only that, how many people could say that on their way to work they passed by a grocery store with two horses hitched to the post out front? Bailey had waved at the two men out for a morning ride. She wished she could have gone along. She hadn't ridden for pleasure in more than a year. These days riding was training, and training helped pay a few bills.

As Bailey got out of the truck, she didn't lock the doors or even take the keys out. She did grab her purse. From across the street a friend she had gone to school with waved and called out her name, asking how Bailey's dad was doing.

Bailey smiled and nodded. She didn't have an answer about

her dad, not today. She hurried down the sidewalk to the front door of the diner, opening it and shuddering at the clanging cowbell that had been hung to alert the waitresses to the arrival of new customers.

"We're expecting the ladies' group from the Community Church." Lacey tossed a work shirt in Bailey's direction as soon as she walked into the waitress station.

"Wonderful, quarter tips and plenty of refills on coffee."

Bailey loved the darlings of the Community Church, but she would have liked a few tables that left real tips, especially today. Real tips would have helped her to forget the call from the mortgage company, letting her know that she was behind—again.

"They specifically asked for you," Lacey informed her as she started toward the coffeemaker.

"Of course they did." They liked to tell her how much they loved her and how they were praying for her.

Bailey closed her eyes and grabbed hold of the cynical thoughts that were dragging her down a dead-end road. She told herself to count her blessings, like the song said. Count her blessings; see what God has done.

So she did. She counted her dad, still in her life. She counted Meg, whose morning hugs made everything better. She counted Lacey and her church family.

Cody's face flashed through her mind, as if God was trying to remind her of something. She squeezed her eyes tightly, but the mental image wouldn't fade. "Okay, God, thank You for Cody."

"What was that?" Lacey walked up behind her, carrying a full pot of coffee.

"Nothing." Bailey washed her hands and reached for the nearly empty ketchup bottles, wondering how they went through so much ketchup during the breakfast rush. Who used ketchup at breakfast?

"You mentioned Cody."

"I was thinking aloud."

"Okeydoke, then, I guess this isn't something you want to talk about."

"No, it isn't."

The bells on the front door clanged, signaling the arrival of customers. Saved by the bell, Bailey flashed Lacey a smile and hurried to the tables that had been set up for the Golden Girls Bible Study.

The ladies—there were ten of them today—were especially chipper and talkative. They were the same ladies Bailey had known all her life, in pastel and floral dresses, cheeks powdered and hair styled twice a week at Ruth's Beauty Shop. These women had been her teachers, librarians, neighbors and friends. These ladies had held a baby shower for her when others had been busy whispering behind their hands.

After bringing their food, Bailey hovered, listening to stories of grandchildren and bad-pet behavior. Every now and then one of the women would motion for her to take a plate or refill a coffee cup.

The diner had started to fill up, and Bailey slipped away to take the orders of her other customers, but she hurried back to the Golden Girls when they motioned for her.

Mrs. Lawrence, once the town librarian, reached for Bailey's hand after the meal and Bible study were over. Her cool fingers wrapped around Bailey's, and she wouldn't let go. Her eyes filled with tears and she shook her head.

"Honey, I've been thinking about you and your daddy and praying for you night and day. You feel like family, I've known you all so long."

Bailey leaned in and hugged the woman. "Thank you, Mrs. Lawrence. We appreciate your prayers."

The other women started to add their condolences. Bailey's eyes filled with tears as she listened to stories about her dad and even her mom when they were young kids.

Bessie Johnston laughed as she reached for her empty cup of coffee and then shot Bailey a hinting look. Bailey hurried to fill the cup.

"You all probably remember this as well as I," Bessie started, "but one of my favorite memories of Jerry Cross is the pie he stole from my windowsill."

Anna Brown was nodding her head so vehemently that Bailey was afraid the woman would lose the pins that held her nest of gray hair in place.

"Yes, I remember. It was Jerry and that Gordon boy. They were out riding horses and causing no end of trouble. They'd just ridden through the clean laundry hanging on my line when they headed toward your place."

"They rode through my hen yard," Jean Forester added. "My hens were scattered in all directions."

"They rode right through my yard, past the window, and they grabbed that apple pie that I'd put on the sill to cool." Bessie chuckled as she told the rest of the story. "I was frying chicken for supper and when I turned around, the pie was gone and those boys was riding as fast as they could down that dirt road."

Jean Forester sighed, "Oh, honey, those were really the good ole days. Remember, we thought those boys was bad. But they weren't bad—they were just boys."

"I remember that when my Eddie got killed after that tractor rolled—" Elsbeth Jenkins wiped her eyes with a handkerchief she pulled out of her sleeve "—it was Jerry that took care of our place for nearly a month. He'd feed his animals and then he'd come and feed ours. And here I've been, sitting at my house wishing I could do the same."

Bailey had been a bystander, listening to the memories unfold as the women of the Golden Girls Bible Study relived a past that Bailey hadn't known about. She took back her mean thoughts about quarter tips and silently asked God to forgive her for her cynicism.

"I'm really glad you all came in today. I'm glad you shared your stories."

"Sweetie, we came to do more than share stories." Mrs. Lawrence reached for her hand again. "Honey, we came to share our hearts. We know that we're not the best tippers in the world, and yet you always give us the best service. You always smile and ask how we're doing, even when you're going through so much."

"I don't mind." Hadn't she minded earlier? Her heart ached.

"Well, we're right sorry about the trouble you all are having and we want to help. So here's our tip, for today's service and for the past when you've been so good to us." Elsbeth Jenkins pushed an envelope into Bailey's hand. "Don't argue with us, Bailey Cross. We're being faithful to God, and if you don't take this, you'll steal our blessing."

Bailey nodded, but her throat tightened, restricting words. Her sweet ladies took turns standing and hugging her and then they gathered their purses and left. And at each of their plates was the customary two quarters that they always tipped.

Without looking in the envelope, Bailey shoved it into her pocket and started to clear the table. Lacey was nowhere to be found as Bailey headed toward the kitchen with the tub of dirty dishes and sloshing glasses of ice water.

"Wasn't that the sweetest thing?" Lacey walked out of the employee's restroom, her eyes red and tearstains on her cheeks.

"It was sweet." It was God showing her something about the people in her life. And it was God showing her something about who He was in her life.

Bailey set the tub of dishes down for Joey, the teenager who came in every afternoon for cleanup. Jolynn and Harry, the owners of Hash-It-Out, had a soft spot for anyone in need and hired nearly anyone who asked for a job.

"I wish I could have grown up somewhere like this."

Lacey had that wistful look on her face again, the one she wore when she thought about the idyllic life of her dreams. That life included growing up on a farm, not in the city—watching her parents fight until the fighting ended with the two going in separate directions and sixteen-year-old Lacey left to her own devices.

Bailey knew that Lacey was saving her tips and working two jobs to buy a place of her own. She wanted a few acres, "bottle calves" and chickens. And she had an absurd dream about finding a cowboy of her own.

"I wish you could have grown up here, too." Bailey hugged her friend. "But if you had grown up here, you wouldn't be you. And I really like you."

"Oh, honey, you're going to make me cry all over again."

"It's true, Lacey. You're unique because of where you came from and what God has done in your life. I know it wasn't easy to get here, but there's a reason for all of it."

Lacey's smile melted. "Don't forget that, Bailey. There's a reason for all of this. There's a reason for what those ladies did for you today. And you might as well accept that the church is having a fund-raiser to help cover some of your dad's medication."

"I know, Lacey. And I am thankful." Bailey walked away, she was thankful, and she knew God had a plan.

It made her wonder if there was a reason for Cody in her life, just when she needed him. He had showed up for one reason, thinking it was for himself that he had to see her.

God had had another plan. Bailey wanted to count that as a blessing, but she didn't know how. Instead it felt like a big test she hadn't studied for.

Chapter Five

Cody stood in the center of the kitchen, trying to come up with the correct expression of parental authority for his young daughter. The problem was, he was struggling not to laugh.

Standing in front of him, her hands with pink painted nails resting on her hips, she looked like the one in charge. Today she was wearing a yellow sundress with her pink boots. Those boots obviously meant a lot to her.

Snapping back into control, he gave her a long look, hoping he could read the truth, or lack of truth, in her stormy-blue eyes. With her lips pursed and her nose wrinkled in disbelief, she looked a lot like Bailey, and she had him nearly convinced she would never try to con him.

"Honest, she said we could have ice cream for lunch."

She had been trying to convince him of this for a good fifteen minutes. He was a novice at parenting, but he was sure a mother who said no to soda probably didn't say yes to ice cream for lunch. He was almost thirty-one years old, he had to be smarter than a five-year-old.

"I tell you what, we'll call your mom at work and ask her about the ice cream."

"I think that would be a bad idea. She doesn't like to be bothered at work." She fidgeted and squirmed, trying hard, it seemed, to avoid looking at him.

"Meg, I really think we need to be honest here. I think your mom would want you to have soup or a sandwich, and maybe ice cream for dessert. If you're honest with me, we'll do something fun later."

Bribery had to be a part of parenting. If it wasn't, well, he could always claim that he didn't know better. It seemed to be working. Meg swayed, swishing her yellow dress back and forth as she worked her mouth and eyed him with deep suspicion.

"Okay, she didn't say ice cream for lunch. But she did buy some chocolate kind with bunnies in it. It has chocolate bunnies."

"Well, I can see how that would be better than a sandwich, but it also wouldn't be too good for us. Now I need for you to be a big girl and help me figure out where everything is. You can be my helper."

She gave him another one of those disbelieving looks and sighed. "You really don't know much about being a dad, do you?"

A five-year-old had figured him out. She had put into words all of his fears and the reason he ran from Bailey in the first place. And he was already doing what his dad had taught him to do, bribing a kid.

He hitched his jeans at the knee and squatted in front of her. She was holding tight to a stuffed bunny that Jerry had bought her two years ago on her birthday. She told Cody that when she woke up. It was then that he had counted the Christmases and birthdays he'd missed. Thinking about it had left a huge hole inside him.

"You're right, Meg, I don't know a lot about being a dad. But I'm going to do my best. And when I do something wrong, I want you to tell me. And I promise I'll listen." He twirled one of her blond pigtails around his finger and she smiled. "And the other thing I can't do is offer you something for being good."

Her mouth dropped at that bit of information. "But it's okay. It's like giving me 'lowances if you buy me something. Especially something like a pony. Or a pet monkey."

A chuckle worked its way up and he had to laugh. "A pet monkey?"

She nodded like it made perfectly good sense to her, and then she leaned closer. "I heard that monkeys are a lot like babies, and that would be almost like a brother or sister."

They were definitely two to nothing, and he was on the losing team.

"Tell you what, we'll think about a stuffed monkey but no bribes. I want you to be good because you are good. And when I buy you something, it'll be because I love you."

"Okay, and then we can have ice cream."

Cody stood up, his knees creaking a protest. It was moments like that—when his joints creaked or when he could barely get out of bed in the morning—when he realized that his career as a bull rider was almost over. He had almost made it to the world championship.

Now, with Meg staring up at him, wasn't the time to dwell on what could have been.

"How about fried bologna for lunch?" He tossed the suggestion over his shoulder as he looked in the fridge.

"Ewww, that would be gross."

He looked behind him and the expression on her face matched the disgusted tone of her voice. "You don't like fried bologna?"

"No, I don't think so. I do like oatmeal."

"Oatmeal for lunch." It seemed reasonable. "What do you like on your oatmeal?"

"She's trying to pull one over on you, Cody," Jerry's voice from the hall interrupted the lunch discussion. Cody waited until the older man walked around the corner into the kitchen before responding.

"So, no oatmeal and no fried bologna?" He shifted his gaze from Jerry to Meg. "Any other suggestion, Meghan?"

"That *isn't* my name." She glared and he knew he was losing ground quickly.

"Sorry, I didn't know." He had felt less pain at the mercy of a fifteen-hundred-pound bull. Gut-stomped didn't begin to describe this moment in his life. He didn't know Meg's complete name, he didn't know the exact date of her birthday and he didn't know what to feed her for lunch.

"We'll have grilled cheese." Jerry made it sound like an easy decision.

Cody shot the older man a look and a smile of appreciation. Jerry winked and sat down at the table, pulling his grand-daughter close.

"And Meg Alice is going to eat her sandwich and then take a nap." Jerry kissed her cheek and she smiled again.

Jerry knew how to be a dad.

The clock on the dash of the truck read 2:45. It had never kept accurate time, so Bailey knew it was closer to three as she pulled to a stop next to the barn and killed the engine. The truck rattled and shuddered a few times after she turned the key.

That couldn't be a good sign.

She glanced toward the house. It appeared to be in one piece, which was more than she felt. Today had been one that seemed to rip her into little pieces of emotional baggage. The Golden Girls had done a number on her, leaving a patch of vulnerability that she hadn't been able to overcome—not even with the sundae covered in hot fudge that Lacey had made her for lunch.

Now she had to go into the house and deal with Cody. To make it even worse, her head ached and she was exhausted. Maybe she could sit in the truck for an hour or so and no one would notice.

No, she couldn't do that. She had dinner to cook and chores that needed to be done. Her gaze carried across the two-acre lawn and landed on the weed-infested garden, which she'd thought was such a good idea in early spring. Her weeding job last week hadn't done a bit of good.

It had given them plenty of tomatoes and quite a few zucchini. Now it was a wonderland for Japanese beetles. The leaves on the green beans were gnawed away, leaving lacy skeletons of green. All in all, gardening was not her thing.

Her gaze shifted to the barn and the mare that was close to foaling. Peaceful, the mare, was the only animal she had left that was broke. Bailey longed to go for a long ride, to put all of her worries aside, if just for thirty minutes.

And she wanted to go inside and find a list of numbers, people who had called and were interested in her horse-training services. The two horses she had would be gone in a month. And then what? That extra thousand dollars a month meant a lot to her family.

Speaking of money. She pulled the envelope of money from her purse. It held enough cash to buy groceries, pay the electric bill and buy school clothes for Meg. Bailey closed her eyes and whispered a soft "Thank You" into the cab of the truck.

She opened her eyes after the brief prayer and looked out the window. Blue had spotted her. The dog trotted across the yard and sat down outside the truck, waiting patiently for some kind of command. Bailey pushed the truck door open and hopped down to the ground. Blue waited, her hind end wagging a nonexistent tail.

"Come on, girl, let's go in the house." The invitation was all the blue heeler needed. She jumped up and started running in circles. The dog wanted cattle to herd; so did Bailey.

The quiet drone of voices reached Bailey as she walked across the porch. Cody's voice and her dad's, blending as they discussed the farm.

"I keep telling her to sell off some of the land." Jerry Cross's voice was weaker than it had been a few days ago.

Bailey thought about his idea to sell, an idea she'd been ignoring for a few months now. It would make him feel better, knowing she had that money. It would make her feel as if she was selling her birthright.

"Maybe we could find another way." Cody shuffled papers. Bailey waited, wondering what they were looking at and what papers Cody had in his hands.

"We've used up all the other ways." Jerry spoke quietly and then continued, "Maybe if you offered to buy a portion of it?"

"I don't think that would be the right move."

Of course he didn't. And Bailey knew why. Having that land, not that she wanted him to have it, would put him in their lives permanently. Cody Jacobs didn't want forever.

"It seems like the only move that makes sense," Jerry answered, sounding about as low on faith as she had ever heard. She didn't want that for him.

Bailey wanted her dad to have peace and to know they were going to survive. And it seemed as if only one thing could give him that peace. She didn't know if she could do that. She didn't know if she could sell her family farm.

She walked into the house, tossing her purse on the counter as she made her way into the living room. The two of them were sitting on the couch, the farm records on the coffee table in front of them. They looked up when she walked in, both with guilty expressions on their faces.

Cody's gaze locked with hers and held. Her dad looked away. Bailey waited, hoping they would offer an explanation. Cody's hands were on the pile of bills, the ledger where she kept records was open in front of him.

They were pushing her out, taking over and making decisions. And she hadn't been involved. Her thin thread of control was being snipped and she was dangling.

"Did you two manage to sell the farm while I was at work?"

"Bailey, we're only trying to come up with solutions. Better to sell and hold on to the house than to have the bank auction it off." Her dad leaned forward, pointing to the pile of bills she'd been trying to juggle paying.

That brought to mind a picture of herself in the center of the room, tossing envelopes into the air, trying to catch them all, and watching them fall all around her. She would never be able to run away and join the circus.

"Did we get any calls from the ad?" She pointed that question in Cody's direction.

"Only one."

Her faith was bottoming out and needed a serious refill. "I need to check on my mare."

As Bailey walked out the back door, her gaze flitted to her purse. How quickly she had forgotten the blessing that had been handed her that day. Maybe it wouldn't solve every problem, but that envelope of money would give her breathing room. She really needed to breathe.

Her mare was standing in a far corner of the corral, her head down and her sides heaving. It wouldn't be long. Or it might be forever. It would take longer if the mare knew she had an audience. Bailey walked into the shadowy barn, feeling more at peace in that quiet place with the scent of horses, hay and cedar shavings.

Alone, she felt the presence of God and that still, small voice that told her heart to trust Him. There wouldn't be big answers or great miracles, she was sure of that, but she was also sure of the peace and the strength He gave her to climb the mountains in the path she had to take.

How could she sell her family farm? She leaned against the rough oak of the doorway to watch the corral and the restless mare. She had called the horse Peaceful because from the day the mare had been born, she had been so calm, so sweet natured.

Trust. It wasn't easy to trust with something as huge as selling the farm. She prayed that God would help her make the right decision. And she would tell her dad she was considering it. She would do that for him, so that he could have peace.

Soft footsteps on the hard-packed dirt floor alerted her to Cody's presence. She knew it had to be him. The steps were sure and steady, accompanied by the light rattle of spurs on his boots. He'd told her yesterday that he was going to ride a few bulls today. He needed to keep in shape.

His hand touched her shoulder, his fingers lightly massaging. Bailey froze with him at her back, her breath catching as he leaned closer, his forehead touching the back of her head, resting lightly as his hands moved to her arms.

"I know I can't make it better, but I do want to help." He whispered the words.

Somehow she shook herself loose from old memories that his touch evoked. Instead she remembered minutes earlier and his easy offer to buy her family farm and then she remembered him, six years ago, walking away from something he thought would tie him down.

"This is helping? I can't rely on temporary fixes and on someone who will only be here as long as it is comfortable to stay."

"I'm here because I want to be here."

Bailey nodded; she didn't know what to say. She could tell him that she knew he wanted to be there. As much as she wanted to deny it, and as much as she wanted to think he was looking for a way out, she could see determination in his eyes. He planned on being in their lives. She also knew how much he wanted that world title. If she could have made the words come out, she would have told him she understood, and she wanted it for him, too.

Words wouldn't come, because her heart wanted something more. She wanted to lean into him and let him hold her for a while. She wanted to stop being strong, just for a few minutes. And no one but Cody made her feel as if she could let her guard down that way.

"Bailey?" He pulled her around to face him, and she let him hold her close because for that moment that was what she wanted.

How long had it been since she'd let herself have something she wanted?

The silent tears rolling down Bailey's cheeks were his undoing. He had come here a week ago to make amends and then to move on with his life, and here he was, holding on to something he couldn't have.

He could count the reasons why this wouldn't work. First and foremost, he was just learning to trust himself to be a person who could be counted on. Second, he had a commitment to sobriety, to wait a year before building new relationships.

Somehow he didn't think his daughter counted in that. That was a relationship that had to be built now.

"Bailey, don't—" He stopped himself from telling her not to cry. Instead he gathered her into his arms and held her close. She didn't fall apart the way he expected. No sobs shook her shoulders.

He lifted her chin with his finger and looked into her eyes, wishing he could know if she felt the soft connection he felt.

"Cody, I…"

If she meant to resist, he didn't know. For a fleeting second he didn't care. Bailey was in his arms and the memories were returning, reminding him of a time when someone had made him feel worthy. Bailey made him feel that way, in a way that no other woman ever had. He didn't understand it, didn't want to figure it out; he just wanted to hold her close and feel that way again—like someone who could be counted on.

He leaned and her lips parted in a silent acceptance. The moment had all of the innocence of a first kiss, soft and tentative, more miraculous than the first breath of spring on a winter's day. Her arms moved to the back of his neck, holding him close, and he felt her rise on tiptoes to bring them closer.

After a long moment he pulled back, moving out of the circle of her arms and swiping his hand through his hair. That had definitely felt like something. She looked like a woman who didn't want to feel something, and he knew she had.

Maybe she had more sense than he did.

"We can't do this," she whispered as she backed away. "I can't let myself go there, Cody, not with Dad and Meg."

"I know." He couldn't tell her about "no relationships" for another five months. A kiss didn't really mean a relationship.

He touched her cheek, letting his fingers rest on the softness, and then he moved, knowing they both needed distance. "I know we can't, and I know we shouldn't. I'm sure not sorry that I did."

But she was sorry and that said it all. She had regret written all over her face, just like six years ago. He didn't want to be the person she constantly regretted letting into her life.

Instead he had to do something he might regret.

"Bailey, I want to buy that hundred-thirty acres. That'll leave you twenty-five and the house."

"I don't want to sell it to you."

"I'm not going to take control of your life."

"It isn't you, Cody. I don't want to sell it, period. And I especially don't want you to buy it just to bail us out." She turned away from him, back in the direction of the laboring mare. A long sigh and her shoulders slumped. "I know that I might have to sell, and I'm going to tell Dad that, because he needs to hear it."

"Let me loan you money." It made perfect sense to him.

"I can't. I don't want to borrow and have one more debt I have to worry about repaying."

"It isn't going to go away, Bailey. Ignoring it all isn't going to make it disappear."

"You think that I don't know that?" She turned again, facing him with eyes bright with tears and frustration. "You've been here a week and you think you know all there is to know about me, my dad and our situation."

"No, Bailey, I'm aware that I don't know it all. The one thing I do know is that you're too stubborn and too full of pride for your own good."

He walked away, leaving her to deal with her issues because he had plenty of his own to work through. He had to figure out how he was going to get himself out of this mess and back in control of his own life.

As he got into his truck, his gaze shifted to the house and the little girl sitting in a lawn chair on the back porch with a big calico cat on her lap and a sleeping blue heeler at her feet. She waved her hand and smiled, the ice-cream argument obviously forgotten.

Her smile was an arrow to his heart, reminding him of why he had stayed in Gibson. He had a daughter and his life was no longer about himself and what he wanted.

From the cavernous recesses of the barn, Bailey watched Cody drive away. She let go of the breath she'd been holding and the warm mush inside her belly—aftereffects of the kiss.

She definitely couldn't linger on the memory of that moment in his arms. Instead she walked back outside to check on the mare.

The mare wasn't going anywhere. She had paced, heaved and then settled in the shade of the barn. Bailey rubbed Peaceful's gray neck and leaned close to inhale the scent of the animal.

"I'll be back in half an hour, sweetie. Please have that baby so I don't have to call the vet."

As she walked across the yard, Bailey saw Meg sitting on the porch with her cat and Blue. The frown on her daughter's face issued a warning.

"Hey, Meggie, how was your nap?"

Meg stood up, dusting cat hair off her yellow sundress. "It was a long nap."

"Maybe the two of us should have an ice-cream cone?"

"Maybe." Meg's eyes narrowed and then watered. "I'm sorry, Mommy, I didn't mean to lie, but I wanted those chocolate bunnies."

Okay, this wasn't the wonderful bonding moment Bailey

had counted on. She pulled her daughter close and hugged her, enjoying the feel of having her near. And then she felt another dose of regret. When was the last time she'd spent a real day with her daughter? When was the last time they'd had fun?

"Meg, we should go to the creek and wade. Maybe we could take a picnic for later, for our supper?"

Meg sniffled. "Even though I lied?"

"What did you lie about?" Bailey sat down on the edge of the porch and pulled her daughter down next to her.

"I told Da—Cody that I could have ice cream for lunch."

"Did he believe you?"

Meg shook her head. Bailey moved onto the bigger issue, the one she would rather not deal with.

"Meg, do you want to call him Dad?"

Meg nodded and held tight to the cat that had crawled back on her lap. "I think he makes a pretty good dad, even if he doesn't get me a pet monkey."

Bailey almost asked about the monkey, but she was afraid she didn't want to hear the explanation. Monkeys, lies about ice cream and Cody being Daddy seemed to be enough for one day.

"Let me check on Grandpa and then we'll drive to the creek. Can you get the fishing poles for us?"

Meg nodded and then she was off and running. Bailey stood and walked into the house. Her dad was still in his recliner in the living room, a glass of iced tea on the table next to him.

"Dad?"

He shifted and turned to face her, the oxygen tube saying more than words about his condition. Bailey mentally pulled herself together and smiled strongly for his sake.

"Dad, I'll put out feelers for selling the hundred acres."

"I'm glad, sis, real glad. And don't be so quick to turn down Cody's offer."

"I'll pray about it."

"I know you will." He leaned back, his eyes closing. "Did I hear you telling Meg you'd take her to the creek?"

Bailey sat down on the arm of the sofa. "Yes. Do you want me to take the truck so you can go with us?"

The way they used to, before he got so bad.

"No, not this time. Maybe in a day or two, when it's cooler."

Bailey nodded, pretending that they both believed he would go fishing again. She stood and leaned to kiss his cheek. "Maybe on Sunday after church?"

"That's a good idea. We can take a picnic."

"I'm taking the walkie-talkie, Dad. And yours is here on the table if you need me."

"I'm just going to watch *Oprah*. You two have fun." He opened his eyes. "Bailey, have fun for Meg's sake. She needs to be a little girl, and you need to be her momma."

Bailey touched his arm as she left the room, his words still hanging in the air around her. Had she let Meg down? He hadn't said that, hadn't even implied it, but now she had to think about the lack of time and attention her little girl had gotten.

She took a few minutes to fill a backpack with junk food and bottled water, and then she walked out the door, smiling for her daughter's sake and determined to make this a good time for the two of them. But as they crossed the yard to the truck, the part of her that was still her daddy's little girl wanted to go back into the house and beg him to hang on, to not let go.

Instead she helped Meg into the truck and then tossed the backpack and poles into the back. They were going fishing and they were going to have fun. They were going to laugh.

"Mom, is Grandpa going to be okay?" Meg leaned out the truck window, her blue eyes more like Cody's than ever before.

"He's going to be okay, today." Bailey stepped close and put a hand on each of her daughter's cheeks and kissed her brow. "But you know that he's going to go to heaven, right?"

Meg nodded. "I know, but I've been praying that Jesus will change his mind."

Meg scooted across to the passenger side of the truck as Bailey opened the door and climbed in. She smiled at her daughter as she turned the key in the ignition.

"Me, too, Meg. Me, too." She remembered almost a little too late to pull herself up by the bootstraps. Meg brought her back to firm footing. "But we have to be willing to accept that God's plans and ours aren't always the same. We have to be willing to let Grandpa go. And we have to know that we aren't going to be alone. God isn't going to forget us. We have to trust that He'll get us through."

"And God brought my daddy to help." Meg said it so brightly, as if it was one of the smartest ideas God had ever had.

Bailey smiled. "Yes, honey, God brought your dad."

And even if she didn't want to see the wisdom of God's plan, and as much as she fought the truth, it felt good to lean on someone.

Chapter Six

Cody leaned against the fence at Jack Brown's place and watched a young bull run past the chute for the second time. The bull had won two out of three rounds against Cody. The last ride had lasted only three seconds.

To make himself feel better, Cody decided to blame his inability to last eight seconds on Bailey. He didn't know if he should blame it on the disagreement over the land, or the way his mind had gotten stuck on the way she felt in his arms.

"He'd make a good bull for you to start with, Cody. I've had him in a few smaller events and he knows what to do. He comes out of the gate spinning."

A good spinning bull that threw in a few bucks and some quick direction changes was exactly what Cody wanted. He would need something to do when he retired from bull riding. And the way things were going, retirement would come sooner than he planned.

"I like him, Jack. He's out of some good bucking stock, and you've done a good job raising him."

"He's a bull you could take all the way to the world finals."

Jack leaned on the opposite side of the fence, not on the same side as the bull, like Cody. Jack loved the sport, but he had never been a bull rider.

"He's definitely the bull I could go places with. And the sport is growing fast."

"Always good to be in on the ground floor. Or as close to the ground as you can get." Jack had been chewing on a long blade of grass. He tossed it now and whistled, waving for his son to move the bull out of the pen. "I want to show you those geldings that I need to have trained. Are you sure she can do the job?"

"Loan me a trailer and I'll take them with me this evening."

"Are you going to stay in Missouri long? I watched on TV the other night, and they were talking about your absence and some speculation that you'll lose the world title over this."

Cody shrugged and let his gaze drift over the two-hundred-acre ranch, a good-size place for this part of the country where grass was more plentiful and could graze more head of live-stock per acre than out West.

He really liked Jack's farm, with its white vinyl fences and the clean lines of the brick ranch house a short distance away. It was the kind of setup that made a guy dream about having a place of his own.

"I heard that Jerry Cross isn't doing very well." Jack reached over the fence to run his hand down the neck of a buckskin gelding that his son had turned into the corral after the bull had finally been penned up.

"He's holding his own."

"And his daughter?"

"Running the show and as strong as that old oak tree out there." Cody reached for the halter of the buckskin as a deep red bay trotted up to the fence. "I like this guy."

"He's for sale."

Cody laughed. "Everything's for sale, isn't it, Jack?"

Jack shrugged at that. "Just about everything. Did you want to ride that bull again?"

Cody shook his head. "I don't think my body would take another throw like the last one."

He'd be paying for that toss for a few days, and then some. He could already feel his joints stiffening and a tight catch in his back. It didn't help that the bull had turned on him, ramming him with horns that had been cut but still did the job.

"Bull riding is a young man's sport."

"Yes, and they're getting younger every year." Raising a few bulls, maybe some horses, was looking better all the time.

"Take the horses with you. If you decide to buy the buckskin, let me know." Jack unlatched the gate and Cody walked through, holding the rail for support.

"I'll take the buckskin, Jack. I'll pay you for him now, and I'll take them both to be trained."

And he'd deal with Bailey's anger. But he had to do something. He'd seen the worry furrowing her brow when she realized there hadn't been any calls on the ad. She needed the income and he could provide it.

Cody's phone rang as he walked toward his truck. He frowned at the caller ID with Chuck Colson's name, and this time he answered. Chuck owned a huge farm-supply business, and it wouldn't do Cody any good to ignore the man who helped pay his bills.

"Cody, I've been trying to reach you." Chuck's voice was deceptively good-natured. "How are you?"

Sober, Cody wanted to reply. He knew Chuck's concern was genuine, but it was about more than Cody's well-being; it was about the name *Colson Farm Supply* that was stitched onto almost every bit of clothing Cody wore into the arena.

"I'm fine, Chuck. I just bought myself a nice buckskin gelding."

"Cody, we need you on tour."

Cody opened the door of his truck and slid behind the wheel, holding the phone with his chin and shoulder. "I know, and I'll be back. Next weekend in Chicago. I'll fly in on Thursday."

"Good, I'm glad to hear that. We'd like to have you stop by the dealership in that area and sign some photographs."

"I'll be there, Chuck."

Long pause. Cody waited for the question that had to come. He knew that Chuck would be straight up; he wouldn't beat around the bush.

"Are you sober, Cody?"

Cody started his truck as he ruminated over that question and how offensive it could have been. It would have been nice to have trust from the people who knew him. But trust had to be earned. He was on the path to earning it but obviously wasn't there yet. He hadn't proven himself.

"I'm sober. I'm helping a friend whose dad is sick."

"Good, I'm glad to hear that. Cody, you know if you need anything…"

"I'd call you, Chuck. And I appreciate that offer."

"Next week, then?"

Yes, next week. He would have to fly out, leaving Bailey, Meg and Jerry behind. Three weeks ago they hadn't been a part of his life. Now he didn't know how to walk out on them.

He told himself he wasn't walking out. He had a career. He had responsibilities, other people who were counting on him. He was three months away from finally being a world champion.

Bailey watched from the creek bank as Meg splashed near the water's edge, grabbing at minnows that swam past her feet.

They had tried fishing, but fishing meant staying out of the water. That was hard to do on a warm summer afternoon, especially for a five-year-old.

"I wish I could have more picnics down here." Meg sat down on the grassy slope near the creek. She moved her hands through the water and then leaned to look at her reflection. "I really do look like him."

She whispered the words as if it was the most miraculous thing of her young life. Maybe it was. Maybe it was a connection that Bailey hadn't realized her daughter needed.

"Yes, honey, you look like him." Bailey opened the backpack and pulled out cupcakes and bottled water. "How about a snack?"

"It might ruin my supper."

"It might, but we don't do this very often, so I think it will be okay."

Meg scrambled up and climbed onto Bailey's lap. "I love you, Mommy." She giggled and wiggled, wrapping wet and slightly muddy arms around Bailey's neck.

"You little rat, you." Bailey kissed Meg's cheeks until a real belly laugh rolled out. "I love you, Meg."

"I love you, too."

"Hey, what does it take to get in on this party?" Cody's voice carried from a short distance away. Blue barked a greeting, not a warning, to the man walking toward them.

"Sorry, this party is by invitation only." Bailey smiled to let him know she was teasing. His grin flashed in return.

"Did you catch any fish?" He pulled a second lawn chair from the back of the truck and opened it next to Bailey's. At close range she noticed the bruise on his jaw.

"Good practice session?"

He shrugged and touched his face. "Yeah, wonderful. I bought a bull."

"You bought a bull?"

"I figured if I couldn't ride him, I should probably own him."

"And is this wonder bull the reason you're walking like a ninety-year-old man?"

"He might have had something to do with it." He shifted and pulled Meg onto his lap. "What about fishing?"

Meg, the little traitor, leaned closely and whispered in his ear, "Mommy doesn't like to touch the worms."

Cody laughed and Meg laughed with him, their heads touching and their smiles matching. "I always knew your mom was a silly ole girl."

"She's not silly—she's just scared." Meg shivered and then laughed again.

"Let me see that pole. I can't ride a mean old bull, but I bet I can handle an earthworm."

Meg handed him the pole and the container of worms. "Do you think we can catch a fish?"

"Now *that* I'm not going to promise. I haven't been fishing in a long, long time." He hooked the worm and cast the line, letting the worm settle to the bottom and then pulled Meg down next to him on the grass bank. Father and daughter. Bailey's heart clenched at the scene.

This is what it feels like to be a family. The thought took her by surprise.

"Do you have another bottle of water?" His question shook her loose from dangerous thoughts that felt like remnants from the past.

Bailey dug into the pack and pulled out a bottle. She unscrewed the cap and handed it to him. He took it with a smile that somehow made everything seem okay.

"Do you want a sandwich?" Bailey reached for the small red

cooler that held their meal. "I made soup for Dad before we headed down here. We're having a picnic."

"Do you mind if I join you? I don't want to barge in on something."

Bailey watched him, sitting next to Meg on the creek bank, helping her hold a fishing pole. She shook her head at the question. He wasn't barging in; he was fitting in. The last felt more dangerous than the first.

"We have plenty."

She made their sandwiches. Cody and Meg ate theirs sitting on the creek bank, the pole resting between them. He told her stories about growing up out West. She told him about the tooth she'd just lost.

The valley grew cool as the sun set behind the hill, leaving the creek and their fishing spot in the shadows of early evening. Pink spread across the horizon, and cicadas began their nightly song. Bailey wanted it to last forever. Every night should be like that one, with Meg laughing and Cody being her dad.

Bailey shooed the thought away because she knew it couldn't happen, and told herself she didn't really want it to, anyway. She had never wanted Cody trapped in her life, against his will.

"You have a foal." Cody's words came out of nowhere as he and Meg were reeling in the fishing pole for the last time.

"I have what!" Bailey jumped up, grabbing her lawn chair and the backpack. "And you're just now telling me?"

He glanced at Meg and then back to Bailey. She got his meaning and she stopped herself, taking a deep breath as she let go of the moment of panic.

"I have a foal." She said it calmly and he smiled, standing up with Meg still in his arms.

"A little gray filly."

"You shoulda told us," Meg whispered into his ear.

"Yes, I should have, but we were having a lot of fun. And the foal is fine. I stayed with the mare, made sure the little girl was eating and I gave her the shot."

"She's okay?" Bailey grabbed both lawn chairs. "They're both okay?"

"They're both okay." He limped to her side, still holding Meg. "Come on, you're not going to believe what else is up there."

"What's up there?" Bailey had a sick feeling as she considered all of the things it could be, and what she didn't want it to be.

A foreclosure notice was at the top of the list.

"I can't tell you—it's a surprise."

"I don't like surprises."

He pushed his hat back and sent an accusing look in her direction. "Neither do I."

Blue jumped in the back of the truck. Meg hurried to the tailgate, as if she thought Bailey wouldn't notice that she was about to climb in the back.

"Where do you think you're going?"

Bailey held her hands out to her daughter, an order to climb down. Normally compliant, Meg this time shot a look at Cody.

"I'll drive slow. She can ride with Blue." Cody stepped in, his face—smooth planes and whiskered cheeks—hidden in the shadows of his hat, but their gazes connected.

Her traitorous mind remembered the firmness of his lips and the way his hands had felt on her back. She gave herself a mental shake and tried to find a way to take back control—of the situation and her daughter.

"She'll be safe, Bailey." Cody's voice was soft, as soft as the southern breeze that slid through the valley.

Bailey caved, and caving was something she had worked

hard against since that summer in Wyoming. Cody smiled, as if he knew that he was the common denominator that equaled her weakness.

She wouldn't let him take over. But Meg was looking at her, wanting so much to be a child with two parents.

"Drive slow, and Meg, sit down on the bottom of the truck bed." Bailey kissed her daughter's cheek.

"I'm proud of you." Cody winked and then opened the driver's side door.

Cody slid behind the wheel of her truck as Bailey climbed into the passenger seat. She glanced over her shoulder to make sure Meg was sitting up near the cab, on the bed of the truck and not on a wheel well. She reminded herself that it was a five-minute drive going less than five miles per hour.

She reminded herself that she had to be strong. She changed the subject.

"Did you check on Dad?"

"He's fine." Cody started the truck and started up the rutted trail toward the house. His hand slid across to hers, his fingers wrapping loosely, but the connection feeling like a strong bond. "Bailey, I don't know when my daughter's birthday is."

The air evaporated from the truck. Bailey rolled the window down and fought back a wave of nausea as that one question bombarded her, making her really think about what she'd done. Her father was the most important person in her life, and she had almost kept Meg from having one of her own.

She could say it was to protect her daughter from someone who might not be a fit parent, but now it looked as if she had been trying to protect herself from someone who didn't want her in his life the way she had wanted, forever.

"March twentieth," she whispered. "Cody, I'm really sorry. I should have told you."

"It's water under the bridge."

"That water can't be brought back. It's five years the two of you have lost."

"We'll manage." He shifted into low gear as they neared the open gate. "I have to leave next week."

Just like that, he undid all of the good thoughts.

"Okay."

"That's all you're going to say?"

"I didn't expect you to stay forever."

He stopped the truck in front of the barn. Bailey looked in the side mirror, watching as Meg and Blue jumped out of the back of the truck and ran to the fence of the corral. The mare was standing with the new foal, the baby still wobbly, but her dark tail wagged as she nursed.

"I have commitments." He was still trying to explain. She tried to listen, but her mind was doing an instant replay of the guy who had said cowgirls always believe they're in love.

Her tumbling thoughts came to a sudden, screeching halt when her gaze landed on the two horses in the front corral and then moved on to the seldom used round pen.

"Why is there a bull in my round pen?" She grabbed the door handle and gave the door a shove with her shoulder. "And where did the horses come from?"

As she walked toward the horses, she heard the jangle of Cody's spurs. She glanced over her shoulder, shooting him a questioning look, which he ignored. The horses, two geldings, trotted up to the fence. The animals moved side by side, and she made a good guess that they were used to being together. He'd brought them from the same place.

The bull had to go. She couldn't have that rangy animal getting loose and getting in the field with her Angus cows.

"Cody?" She reached out and the buckskin gelding, with his

almost dappled yellow coat and black mane and tail, nudged at her hand, his velvety soft lips moving along her fingers for a treat that didn't exist.

"Jack Brown wanted to know if you had time to train a couple of horses. And the bull is on his way to join my herd in Oklahoma. Willow Michaels is picking him up next week on her way through Missouri."

"Gotcha." And she despised the odd emotion twisting at her heart and feeling a lot like jealousy. Willow Michaels was the most beautiful woman Bailey had ever seen. She was tall, slender and had honey-blond hair that hung to her waist. And her friends called her Will. Like having a man's name detracted from her appeal. Bailey knew this all secondhand from interviews she'd seen on TV.

"You don't mind, do you?" Cody hitched up his jeans and lifted his foot to rest on the bottom rail of the corral. "I won't be here to help load him."

"I know you won't. I can handle it."

"Will is a great person. If you haven't met her, you'll love her."

"I've seen her on TV, and I believe the consensus is that everyone loves Will."

"Because she's a nice person."

Bailey nodded but she wouldn't say another word, not with her eyes turning from brown to green and Cody staring at her with a silly grin that added depth to his dimples.

She absolutely was not jealous of Willow Michaels. She turned away from the barn, forgetting to say goodbye until she was nearly to the corral, where Peaceful was nuzzling her new foal. It was too late, then. She glanced over her shoulder and saw Cody talking to Meg. They were petting the buckskin and her daughter was giggling.

Next week he would be gone. They would deal with that when it happened, not today when Meg was laughing like a five-year-old ought to laugh.

The thud of the barn door was Cody's first warning that Bailey had noticed the work he'd done that morning. He hadn't known what else to do. It was Saturday, the feed store was open only until noon, leaving a limited window of opportunity to get something accomplished. They had needed grain and fencing for the back fence or Jack Brown's horses would be out and running down the highway.

Next to him, Meg moved, drawing him back to the picnic table under the shade of the oak tree next to his RV. The laptop in front of him had switched to the screen saver, and his daughter was antsy. He turned his attention back to the business of shopping, knowing that Bailey was heading their way.

"Do you think she's going to be mad?" He asked his daughter as she sipped on the chocolate milk he'd poured for her.

"Pretty sure." Meg peeked back over her shoulder. "Yep, she's mad."

"At me, remember that, not at you."

"Okay." Meg pointed to a dress and he clicked the option to send the size and style to his shopping cart.

The virtual shopping cart full of clothing was a pretty good feeling. It felt almost as good as the two horses in the corral. Bailey might be upset with him, but he'd watched last night when she went out to work the animals, starting them in a circular pattern on the lunge line, and then brushing them until they had nearly followed her to the house for more attention. At least she wasn't sorry to have the horses to train.

He wasn't about to tell her the buckskin was his, or maybe he would give it to Meg. A shadow fell over the picnic table.

"What are you up to now?" She sat down across from him. Her smile softened the words. For a moment, he thought about being in her life like this forever.

"Meg and I are shopping."

"For?"

"School clothes," Meg answered, her tone chipper. He would have picked a different tactic. He might have tried a quieter, less enthusiastic approach.

"That's great, sweetie."

Surprised, he looked up, making eye contact with the woman across from him. She didn't look angry. Her eyes were soft, focusing on her daughter.

"We're almost done. Time to check out." Cody pointed for his daughter to hit the correct button as he pulled his wallet out of his back pocket. "Your dad told me about the BBQ fundraiser at the church tomorrow night."

He typed in his credit card number as he waited for Bailey to answer. When he looked up, she was staring off into the distance. He cleared his throat to get her attention. When she turned, her attention fell first on her daughter and then on him.

"Meg, why don't you go check on the kittens? Their eyes are open and they're starting to crawl around the feed room."

Meg was off and running before another word could be said. It made Cody wonder if she had sensed her mother's mood and wanted to escape, or if she really was that excited about the kittens.

He picked up the insulated carafe of coffee and one of the disposable cups out of the bag. When he set the cup in front of her, she nodded and he filled it. That went well, so he moved on, hoping to persuade her that his help was something she could accept.

Maybe she thought help from him meant ties, or owing him something?

"I wanted to get some things done around here before I left. I hope you didn't mind."

She shook her head, the light breeze catching the feathery strands of her hair. When she looked up, her brown eyes were dark with emotion.

"I don't mind. I've given up minding." She breathed in and let it out in a sigh, a light shake of her head shifting blond hair off her shoulders. "I appreciate your help, Cody."

"Then what's wrong?"

"Meg loves you, and I love her. I don't want her to be hurt. I know how close you are to the world title, and I know how much it means to you…."

He lifted his hand to stop her. "You obviously know how much everything means to me, and yet you don't know how much Meg means to me."

"Cody, I'm sorry."

He closed his laptop and stood up. "I'm sure you are, but you have to trust me. You didn't let me finish what I was trying to tell you yesterday."

"Okay, finish. You were telling me that you're leaving. That's when I saw the bull and the horses."

Cody leaned, resting his hands on the top of the table, and forcing her to make eye contact. "I'm coming back."

She nodded but looked away, which answered his trust question. Could he blame her?

"Okay, you're coming back."

"And right now, I give up. I can't convince you and I'm not going to argue. I'm going to work on that back fence, which is something I *can* fix." He grabbed the work gloves he'd dropped on the picnic table and the bottle of water he'd taken out of the freezer.

As he pulled on the gloves, he remembered telling her that he'd call that summer after Wyoming. And after he left, he hadn't. Not because he hadn't wanted to, but because he'd been afraid to hear her voice, and afraid of what she'd make him feel. He didn't want her to know that.

While he'd been distracted by the past, she had stood and she faced him now, a cowgirl in faded denim and a pink T-shirt, her blond hair framing her face.

"I'll help."

"No, I'd like to do this alone. You should spend time with your daughter, and with your dad."

"Now you're telling me how to be a mom?"

He couldn't win this one. "No, I'm telling you that I can take care of this and you should take care of more important things."

What he couldn't tell her was how he needed distance from her to get his thoughts straight. He couldn't leave at the first of the week with Bailey on his mind. He couldn't ride bulls distracted by thoughts of strawberry lip gloss and brown eyes that looked into his heart. What he could do was work on the farm, and tomorrow he would attend a fund-raiser for Jerry.

Chapter Seven

The four of them rode to town in Cody's truck. Bailey felt her heart grab as they pulled into the parking lot of the small church at the edge of Gibson, the church that Bailey had attended since her birth.

The building had been added onto and now boasted the traditional white sided sanctuary with a bell tower, and at the back was a brick addition that housed classrooms. Old and new blended together, making everyone happy. Most of the time.

Bailey had new thoughts today, thoughts about the coming weeks and months, and about attending church without her dad. And today, attending with Cody, who had been seen, but no one really knew who he was.

Or maybe some had guessed.

Since she'd come home from Wyoming, she had dealt with the embarrassment and the shame of what had happened with Cody. In time the gossip had waned, people had moved on with their lives and with new gossip. Bailey had resumed her roll in the church as someone respected and loved. Meg had been welcomed with loving arms.

Now it was all back, the past had become present.

As Bailey walked next to her dad, Meg holding his other hand and Cody behind them, it was obvious that the rumor mill was working round the clock. A few people stared, and there were carefully averted glances that were less noticeable.

Heat crawled up her cheeks and she slowed her pace.

"What's up, pumpkin?" Her dad's hand tightened on hers. He stopped to take a breath, and she tried to ignore the ashen gray of his complexion. She couldn't, not anymore. And for him she would accept help. The money earned tonight was for him.

"Nothing's up, Dad. I thought maybe you'd like to rest."

"I'm fine. And don't try to fool me. You know I can tell a fib from a thousand feet away."

She leaned against his shoulder and sighed. "Yes, you've always known how to read me."

"Don't let it get to you."

Cody moved closer. Bailey tried to smile at him, but once again he was the reason she felt like hiding. Not that she could blame it all on him. She'd been a partner in that moment six years ago.

"I see Pastor John, I'm going to head that direction and to that lawn chair he's a pointing to." Jerry pulled free, kissing her on the cheek before he walked away.

Bailey let him go, aching to help him but not wanting to point out his weakness. He walked with slow, determined steps, stopping occasionally to rest. When he finally reached Pastor John and the promised seat, Bailey allowed herself to look away.

"Mom, I'm going, okay?" Meg jumped up and down next to her. "I'm going to swing with Katy."

Bailey nodded.

Meg was off and running. Bailey watched as her daughter ran to the swings and a group of children who were calling for her to join them. At least Meg didn't feel it. She was five and hadn't felt the sting of gossip.

Only once had she come home from a friend's house, crying because a little girl at the birthday party had teased her because she didn't have a daddy.

"What's up?" Cody stood next to her, his hair still damp from a shower. He smelled like an Irish spring and cinnamon gum.

"Nothing's up."

"You're acting a lot like that dog of yours when she skirts around the hooves of the horses trying to keep from getting stepped on. Is there something that I don't know about?"

"I'm sorry, Cody, but I can't face this again."

"Face what?"

"Gossip."

She glanced around the picnic area, an acre of grass, swings and tables. She didn't have to look far to see small crowds looking her way, their lips moving. Of course they could have been talking about how she was holding up. Or maybe they were only trying to figure out where she'd come up with a man.

"So, we tell them that I'm Meg's dad. End of story."

She laughed at his innocence. "Oh, come on, you should know better than that. That will only be the beginning of the story. And from the way people are looking at us, the story started before we got here."

"Do you want me to leave?"

Did she? What did he mean by leave? What she wanted was for him to be gone, taking remnants of her past with him. She glanced in the direction of Meg and knew that the past was always with her. And as much as she regretted her mistake, she didn't regret her daughter.

For Meg, she had to allow Cody into their lives. No, she didn't want him gone. She couldn't lie to herself and say that it was all about wanting him in Meg's life.

"Sometimes I don't know what I want."

He laughed, "That makes two of us. I don't know what you want, either. And so, if you don't mind, I'm going to join your dad and Pastor John. I've met him at the diner, and he seems like my kind of guy. He knows that people aren't perfect."

"Cody, I know that, too. And I don't expect you to be perfect. I don't know if you understand that this is more than I can deal with right now. My focus, as you pointed out yesterday, needs to be on Dad and Meg. But with you next to me…"

"Good to know you can't think or focus when I'm around." He bent his head and for a moment she thought he might kiss her. "I'll give you space to think."

Bailey nodded and watched him walk away, Wranglers, a red plaid shirt open with a T-shirt underneath, and the casual swagger of a cowboy. She remembered a little too late that Willow had recently been seen on his arm. Willow, who always looked perfect. Willow, who would be showing up in a few days.

"What's got you working yourself over, talking under your breath like a crazy woman?"

Bailey smiled at Lacey, relieved to have an ally.

"Where've you been?"

"Making my rounds. I walked from the Hash-It-Out. You know that the kids from the agriculture class auctioned themselves off a bit ago, and the money is for your dad. A few of the people who bid are volunteering the kids to work at your place."

"I didn't know." Her heart squeezed at that bit of kindness when just minutes ago she had been worried about what people were saying behind her back.

"It's true. That should make you happy, sweetie. So why do you look so blue?" Lacey wrapped a comforting arm around her and squeezed Bailey's shoulder. "Is that cowboy messing up your oatmeal again?"

He stood next to her dad, the red of the shirt a stark contrast to his dark skin and black hair. He had a can of soda, and someone had given him a plate of food. Pastor John pointed to an empty chair and Cody sat down.

"He isn't bothering me." Not really.

"Okay. You know, people are always going to talk, Bay. Remember how they wore out the topic of my hair when I dyed it black and got the red streaks?" Lacey's smile disappeared. "And you have a man that they don't know living out at your place."

"I questioned the black-and-red hair myself. But it looks good." Bailey laughed. "And they had more fun with the nose ring."

"Cowboy in an RV," Lacey reminded.

"I know."

"So, set people straight or send that cowboy on down the road."

"He's Meg's dad."

Silence. Lacey looked from Cody to Meg, and then back to Bailey. For some reason, Bailey had assumed her friend would guess, or at least have a clue. The stunned silence meant she hadn't thought of the connection.

"I didn't know." Lacey stared in Cody's direction. "I mean, I knew he was someone from your past. But now that you mention it, Meg has his eyes. And you've got a serious problem, because I bet you thought you were over him."

"I am over him. And he won't be here much longer. He stopped to talk and…"

"He stayed. And that's what broke brother Bill's balloon."

"What?" Bailey could never follow a conversation with Lacey. And that reminded her, hadn't she just been considering Lacey an ally?

"Sorry, I think that was a kid's picture book I read one time. A whole set of calamities, and it all ends with one little balloon getting busted. Anyway, it would probably be good if he went on down the road, because then people could let it rest."

"There's nothing to talk about."

"There will be once they figure out he's Meg's daddy."

Bailey ran a hand over her face and shook her head. She didn't need this. She didn't need another problem to solve. And the problem at hand had tossed his plate in the trash barrel and was walking in her direction.

"Well, I hate to skip out on you, but I think they want me to serve pie." Lacey patted Bailey's shoulder as she backed away. "Love ya, sweetie."

"It feels like love." Bailey called out to Lacey, who was laughing as she walked away.

"Small-town life is always a joy, isn't it?" He hooked his arm through hers. "Would you like to do the cakewalk?"

Bailey glanced in the direction of the parking lot, where a circle had been taped off and music was playing as a crowd went around the circle, stepping from numbered square to numbered square.

"The cakewalk would be great. I could use some chocolate." And she didn't even pull her arm loose from his.

"What are we going to do about the talk?" he asked.

"Maybe you should do the right thing and marry me." She regretted the joke immediately. "I'm sorry, that was supposed to be funny."

"I almost laughed." He did chuckle and Bailey sighed.

"I'm sorry, Cody."

"No, I am. I'll be back in a week and I'll move the RV. If I'm gone, they won't have a reason to talk."

In a week he would leave. She should feel relieved. If she thought about it for a few minutes, she was positive relief would surface.

Cody heard the deep sigh and felt Bailey move a step away from him. He would move his RV. That should give her peace of mind, not cause a buildup of tension. He tugged her close and she relented, her shoulder touching his.

"I'm not ashamed of my daughter, Bailey. I want people to know that I'm her father. I understand if you're not ready to tell everyone."

In answer, she shrugged.

Silence hung between them. He looked down and saw that her eyes were on Meg, running across the large lawn, holding the hand of another little girl. The two girls were heading toward the crowd that had gathered on the parking lot where they were holding the cakewalk. Cody, with Bailey at his side, continued to move in the same direction.

A local band had set up on a flatbed trailer, and a country gospel song, a little heavy on the guitar, covered the other noises. The fund-raiser for Jerry had turned into a festive gathering of friends and neighbors, all with the same goal—to help one of their own.

Cody hadn't felt that sense of community until he joined the pro bull-riding tour. And then when he first went to the church services with Jason and some of the other riders.

Those guys had become his first real family following the loss of his grandfather, when he was just a kid a little older than Meg.

Bailey pulled him to a stop fifty feet short of reaching Meg. He saw her gaze dart quickly to her daughter and then back to him.

"Cody, I don't mind if people learn who you are. Meg needs you in her life. She shouldn't have to be the little girl without a daddy."

"No, she shouldn't be that little girl." He wanted her to have everything, including him, in her life. He wanted to be there for her when she needed him. "I don't want to make things difficult for you."

"How bad could it get? The worst was when I came home that summer. This is just leftovers."

"Sometimes leftovers are the hardest to swallow. Especially if it wasn't that great the first time around." He moved his hand to hers and felt her fingers clasping his.

"I can handle it, Cody. I just don't want it to hurt Meg."

"We won't let it."

They reached the crowd at the edge of the parking lot. A line had already formed for the cakewalk on the pavement. He dug into his pocket for money that he handed to a teenager.

"Three of us."

The girl tried to hand him his change, but he shook his head. This was for Jerry and Bailey's peace of mind. And it was for himself, to ease the guilt he felt each time he thought of her carrying a burden that had been partly his.

It didn't sit well, the fact that—like his dad—he was trying to buy an easy conscience. He shuffled those thoughts away as he led Bailey forward.

"You're going to do the cakewalk?" Bailey laughed as he stepped onto the square and pulled her to the one in front of him. From across the circle Meg squealed and ran toward them. Her arms came up and Cody grabbed her and lifted her to his shoulders.

The teenager in the center of the circle hit Play on an ancient cassette player, and praise music, tinny sounding and unable to compete with the band, started to play. As the music continued and they walked around the circle, Cody knew that this was what family felt like. He could even see that this was how a family looked.

As they walked to the wavering music, he glanced around, noticing with envy the way fathers walked with their children or stood in line to shoot baskets for prizes. Those men seemed to know and understand the role of fatherhood and what was expected of them.

Bailey, Meg and he were three pieces but not a whole. He didn't know that he could make them anything different.

"Cody, the music stopped." Bailey pushed him back as he nearly ran over her.

"Sorry, I wasn't paying attention." Longing for something he had never had, never thought he wanted, inched into his heart.

"I know, you stepped on my heel." She smiled, a teasing smile.

The teenage girl called a number. His number. Bailey pulled him in the direction of a table of cakes. His first cakewalk and he'd won. On his shoulders, Meg bounced and laughed. He lifted her off his shoulders when they reached the table.

"Which one do you want?" he asked his daughter.

Meg was already reaching for one with pink icing. It matched her cowboy boots, worn today with a denim skirt and a pink T-shirt.

"We'll take that one." He pointed and the woman behind the table handed over the cake. He tried to pretend he didn't notice the gleam in her eyes as she looked from him to Bailey to Meg.

"We should go check on Dad." Bailey shifted away from the

table, and away from him. Her cheeks were stained with pink and her eyes bright with tears.

She probably wanted him gone. He wasn't ready to leave.

After a Monday that somehow turned into the stereotype of what Mondays were supposed to be, and not in a good way, Bailey walked onto the back porch that evening for the quiet she'd been craving since the picnic the previous day. With her dad and Meg both in bed, this was her time.

Velvety darkness and sultry air blanketed the countryside, and millions of stars twinkled in the inky-black sky. As Bailey sat down with her glass of iced tea, she sighed with relief, feeling totally cut off from the world. That's exactly what she wanted to feel at that moment.

As she sat curled up in a cushioned patio chair, cocooned by the dark night and country silence, she didn't relax. She didn't find the peace she had sought. Instead her mind replayed an earlier conversation with Pastor John, when he had called to tell her that the gossip would fade and that the people who mattered knew the truth—that Cody was living on the property to help out.

On the whisper of a soft breeze a quiet thought returned, a reminder of grace, and forgiveness. The words had been her father's when she had gone to him in tears to tell him she was pregnant.

This, too, shall pass, her dad had said. And the words meant the same today as they did then. This, too, would pass, and soon Cody would be gone. But not really. This new Cody, the grown-up version, didn't appear to be ready to walk away from his daughter.

And that meant she would now have to learn to deal with him in her life on a permanent basis. In her life, but not. More like he was visiting her life, hanging out on the periphery. The most important thing was that he made a real move into Meg's life.

Sort of. If she was trying to fool herself, she could believe it was all about Meg and Cody, and that her own heart had nothing to do with it.

As her mind cleared, her attention wandered and her gaze went with it, in the direction of Cody's RV. The lights in the living area glowed soft yellow through the closed curtains and a faint melody drifted across the lawn.

Forget Cody. She closed her eyes, intending to make good on that. Meg started school next week. Bailey sighed and leaned back in her chair. That was one more thing she wasn't ready to deal with, her little girl going to school.

The door of the RV clicked. She opened her eyes as a shaft of light split the darkness of the yard. Cody stood in the doorway, not yet realizing that she was watching. He slid a hand through his hair and glanced around, obviously upset about his own life and his own problems.

It couldn't have been easy for him. He'd come here to do the right thing; she had to give him that. And look what he'd landed in the middle of. He suddenly had a family, and she knew that family was the last thing Cody wanted. What she didn't know was why.

He stepped down from the RV, pushing the door closed behind him. Blue jumped up from her place on the porch and trotted across the lawn to join him. That's when he saw her. He cocked his head and stared into the dark, and then he raised his hand in greeting and headed in her direction.

Her heart did a loud ka-thump in her chest, almost like the first time she'd seen him back in Wyoming, with eyes that sparkled and a mischievous grin that tied her heart in knots.

So much for the peaceful country night.

Did he know that people paid for noise machines that imitated nights like this, with the sound of the creek in the distance, the chirrup of the cicadas and occasional call of the whippoorwill?

She had the peaceful noises, and she'd been seeking a peaceful feeling to go with them. She and God had almost cleared up a few misunderstandings, and she'd even started to deal with the check from the church, which had felt a lot like charity.

Her dad had reminded her that of the three—faith, hope and charity—charity was the greatest. And how many people could say that enough people loved them to give the way the people of Gibson had given to them?

Cody looked like a man seeking peace, too.

He looked plain drawn out, the mischievous grin no longer in place. He stepped onto the porch and then hesitated, as if he wasn't sure of his place in her world. She couldn't help him with that.

"May I sit down?"

"Of course you may."

He smiled at that, his grin one-sided and landing in her heart. "Really?"

Really? She nodded and motioned for him to sit.

Cody sat down in the chair next to hers, sighing as he settled, stretching his legs in front of him. He had changed into khaki shorts and a white button-down shirt. She wondered where her cowboy had gone.

Blue nudged his hand and he rubbed her ears. When he didn't say anything, Bailey leaned back to relax. Sort of.

But who could really relax with that man sitting next to them. A woman made of stone, maybe. Bailey wanted to be that woman, but she wasn't. She was older, wiser, but still a woman.

"I'm sorry that I have to leave tomorrow."

And that's what broke brother Bill's balloon. Or something like that. Anyway, it was enough to shake her loose from the soft enchantment of a summer night.

"I know that. And I know that Willow will be here in a couple of days to get the bull."

He tilted his head and glanced in her direction. "Bailey, I'm sorry if it feels like I'm running out on you."

This all felt strangely familiar. Hadn't she heard the same thing six years ago?

"You aren't running out on me. You have a life and a career. You have a chance to win something you've dreamed of for as long as I've known you. Or when I knew you."

Another sigh and he tipped his head back. Her gaze followed his to the slow-spinning blades on the overhead fan.

"The world title suddenly doesn't seem so important."

"Don't regret, Cody. You can't get this back."

"There's always another year." He leaned forward, his arms resting on his knees.

Bailey's hand hovered above his back, and she thought about regret and moments you can't take back. Things that couldn't be undone. She moved her hand back to the armrest of her chair.

"There's more to this, isn't there?" Her question brought him back into her presence.

He leaned back again. Blue, at his side, nudged him for attention and his hand settled on her neck.

"I'm just struggling. I didn't think I would. I thought I would quit drinking, go to an AA meeting or two, pray and be suddenly cured."

And she hadn't realized her question would bring such an honest answer. She didn't have time to form an answer; Cody turned toward her, his smile hesitant.

"So much for being in each other's lives, huh?" He brought his left leg up to cross it over his knee, grimacing with the motion. "I'm an alcoholic. I can't undo that or make the facts different. I can't go back and be the person you wanted me to be six years ago. I'm working hard to be the person I want to be."

She shook her head, still praying for wisdom and knowing that God had answers that she didn't. "I'm not asking that from you. We're here today, and we are who we are. Now we have to find the answers for the situation we're in."

"This last seven months or so has been one continuous string of events that I hadn't expected."

"Like learning that you have a daughter?" She thought about it now, what that must have done to someone who was trying to build a new life. "I keep saying I'm sorry, and that isn't going to fix anything. I hope you do know that I mean it."

"I know you are, and I forgive you. I'm still working on forgiving myself."

"It isn't easy—I know from experience. But I also know that God's forgiveness is complete. He doesn't hold on to our past, using it to taunt us or make us feel guilty." She rested her hand on his arm, wondering why that contact with him made her breathe deeper and feel a little calmer. "And the struggle with alcohol isn't going to go away, not overnight, and maybe not ever."

He nodded, his eyes closing. "I know. Right now I feel a lot like Jesus must have felt when he had been in the wilderness for forty days and was being tempted by the enemy."

"He promised He wouldn't give us more than we can handle." She moved her hand from his. "But the key to that is that we aren't supposed to try and handle it alone. We have to lean on Him."

"I'm not sure what I was thinking back in Wyoming."

"What do you mean?"

"I shouldn't have walked away from you. I didn't realize then that women like you don't come along every day."

Bailey's insides quaked as his words registered. When she didn't respond, he reached for her hand and she felt strong fingers wrapping around hers. Men like Cody didn't come along every day, either. She wanted to tell him that, but she couldn't let herself move that far into his life, not yet.

Keeping it about Meg made it easier to deal with him in her life. But hiding behind a five-year-old wasn't really fair.

"Cody, you're stronger than you think. And the way you've stayed here with us. I want you to know that it means a lot to me. You could have left but you didn't."

"Thank you, Bailey." He leaned toward her, still holding her hand, and his lips grazed hers. "Thank you."

"I need to go to bed. I have to work tomorrow." She stood, and he released her hand.

"I'm sorry, I shouldn't have done that."

"I can't go back, Cody."

"That isn't where I'm planning on going." He stood next to her. "I'm only planning to move forward from this point."

"I have so many things to deal with right now." In football she thought they would call this a fumble; she really felt like she was fumbling. She slid past him to the door. "Take care of yourself."

"You, too."

And she walked away from him, when walking away was the last thing she wanted to do. What she wanted, he couldn't give. He couldn't tell her what the future held or where he would be next month, or even next year.

Chapter Eight

Cody pulled up in front of the store, next to Bailey's truck. He needed a few things for the trip. He didn't know if he needed them badly enough to face Bailey after last night. And then again, he wasn't a coward.

He walked into the store, which had probably been a fixture in Gibson since the early 1900s. It still boasted a wood facade, hardwood floors and only four aisles. It smelled like produce, lemon oil and pine cleaner.

Mr. Hastings, the owner, smiled from behind the meat counter, and Mrs. Hastings scurried toward him, wiping her hands on the apron she always wore. Her smile was huge and her eyes were twinkling. Cody suddenly wished he had driven on by and waited until he had gotten to Springfield for the things he needed. Springfield had stores where a person could shop with anonymity.

"Why, Cody Jacobs, we're so pleased to hear the news."

He wondered what news, and he wondered where Bailey had gone to. A giggle from the aisle with canned vegetables and baking supplies answered his question. Whatever was about to go down, Bailey obviously thought it was pretty amusing.

He had a feeling he wouldn't.

"Mrs. Hastings, what news would that be?"

She laughed and patted his arm like she'd known him forever. "Why, honey, we heard about the wedding. We're all so tickled that you're going to do the right thing and marry our little Bailey."

Marry Bailey? He opened his mouth to reply but he couldn't. Marry Bailey? He heard her laughing now. Mrs. Hastings heard it, too, and her smile grew.

"Well, now, I forgot she came in a bit ago. I bet you're looking for her."

"Actually, I…"

"Bailey, come on out—your man is here." Mrs. Hastings gave him a look. From the meat counter, Mr. Hastings, obviously sympathetic to Cody's plight, coughed and cleared his throat. Mrs. Hastings ignored him. "Now, I want the two of you to know that we're going to throw you a wonderful reception at our place on the river."

"Mrs. Hastings, there…"

"Don't argue." She smiled, as if she knew he was trying to set her straight, and she wasn't going to hear it. "Oh, there's Bailey."

Yes, there was Bailey. She pushed a cart around the corner, and his heart tripped all over itself as if maybe she was the one. Blond hair and the face of an angel—what guy wouldn't look at her and feel the same way?

"Cody, I didn't know you were going to be here. Honey."

He couldn't believe she was playing along with this. Had he entered some strange dimension where Bailey played practical jokes? Or had the whole town gone crazy. What if they kept him here, forcing him to marry the woman he'd done wrong?

It could happen. He'd seen movies like that.

"Bailey. I knew you were gone. I thought you were at work."

"No, I'm staying at home with Dad today and tomorrow. After that a few of the women from the church are going to pitch in and help."

"I'll be back as soon as I can. Maybe next Sunday night, if I can fly out that soon."

"No hurry, we'll be fine." She had pushed her cart to the one register and was piling her groceries on the counter.

Cody held his debit card out to Mrs. Hastings. She laughed and didn't take it.

"We don't take plastic, just checks and cash, the way it was intended to be," she explained.

Intended to be? He didn't even want an explanation for that.

Bailey pulled her checkbook out of her purse and shot him a sweet smile. Okay, this was definitely some parallel universe. Shouldn't she be furious about the rumor that they were getting married?

He started to get a little itchy on the inside, like an allergic reaction he'd once had to walnuts. What if Bailey was in on the conspiracy?

What if it was something like the town of Stepford? They were going to clone him and turn him into a good man, the kind who knew how to be a father and a husband. The kind who never made mistakes.

Bailey paid for her groceries, and he picked up two of the paper bags to carry out for her. She followed with the last. As they walked out the door, she growled.

Now *that* was the Bailey he knew.

"What in the world is going on?" He set the bags on the floorboard of the truck and closed the door. Bailey stood next to him, her eyes squeezed shut but a tiny smile quivering on her lips.

"I'm not sure, but I'm going to get to the bottom of it. Seems someone at the picnic overheard us talking about getting married."

"Wasn't that a joke?" He had thought it was, when she said he should do the right thing and marry her.

"It was a joke. Do you really think I want you to marry me?"

She didn't have to stomp all over his ego and act as if it was the last thing she wanted. "No, I didn't think you were serious."

"Someone did and the entire town knows, and they're planning our wedding."

Now what? He leaned against the truck, not caring about the dust or what people driving by would think. "Should we get married?"

She hit him on the arm. "That is the last thing on my mind at this point. Especially to someone who so obviously doesn't want to be married. I want to marry someone who loves me and wants to be with me forever. Remember, cowgirls always think they're in love. Well, we also think it should be forever."

He rubbed the back of his neck and thought about how much easier it was to get stomped by a bull than to deal with an angry female. There were similarities between the two. Both could attack from behind and when you least expected it. Both could be perfectly docile one minute and out for blood the next.

Both seemed to have it out for cowboys.

"You know, Bailey, contrary to popular belief, cowboys feel the same way about love and forever. In our case, there's a little girl involved, and I want to do what is best for her."

"I'm not sure what the answer is to that. I've been trying to do the best thing for her for about six years."

"Well, you're going to have to cut me some slack if I don't have your parenting experience. Remember, I just found out that I'm a dad."

He caught a movement in the window of the store and groaned. Could it get any worse?

"What?" Bailey was looking at him, her back to the store.

"We're being watched. They think either it's a lover's spat or we're talking about wedding plans."

"It's neither, and I'm tempted to go tell them that."

"I wouldn't. Let it die down. When people don't get their invitations, they'll figure it out."

"When your RV is gone, they'll figure it out."

Her big eyes were full of hurt, fresh or from the past, he wasn't sure which. He didn't know how to make things right.

"Bailey, give me a chance to think this through. Give me a chance to do the right thing."

She nodded and turned away from him. He couldn't let her go like that. He couldn't let her walk away with anger between them.

He reached for her hand and pulled her back to him. Before either of them could react or think it through, he leaned, brushing his lips across hers. He lingered in the kiss for just a minute, the way he'd wanted to do last night.

For that minute he wanted to stay forever.

Bailey pulled back, her eyes wide with shock and anger.

"That wasn't the right thing to do, Cody."

"It felt like it in the moment." He brushed the back of his hand across her silky cheek. "See you in a week."

She walked away angrily and he let her go, because he was pretty sure her anger was just an act. And he knew that he had been sober for only seven months and needed a few more under his belt before he pursued a relationship.

The buckskin quivered as Bailey slid the saddle onto his back, but he didn't buck or sidestep. That was the way she had planned it. In the four days after Cody had left, she'd worked with the horses when she could.

She'd taken it easy with the buckskin, getting him used to her touch, to her leaning on his back and to the smell of the leather. And the creak of the saddle. She had learned that lesson a few years earlier, when she'd dealt with a horse that had been terrific until the saddle creaked under her weight.

She never would have thought about that sound being the undoing of a horse. Now she thought about it each time a storm hovered on the horizon and her bones ached, a remnant of the fall she'd taken.

The buckskin was a baby and leaned against her as the saddle settled onto his back. He wanted to be comforted during this strange new process.

"Big Baby, that should be your name. I think I'll recommend that when they come to get you." She rubbed his neck and whispered that if she could, she would keep him.

"Mommy, look at the big trailer."

Bailey pivoted and the horse shied, sending the saddle to the ground and further scaring him. He jumped away from her, jerking the leather reins from her hands.

"Easy, fella." she reached for the reins and the horse moved again, his eyes rolling wildly.

Meg ran across the yard, her pigtails flapping. That didn't help. The horse turned to see what the new danger was and his hoof came down on Bailey's heel. She bit down on the scream and blinked furiously to clear her vision. The truck and cattle hauler had rumbled to a stop a short distance from the corral.

"Mom, are you okay?" Meg whispered in a loud voice from outside the pen.

"I'm fine, honey, just a little sore." Nothing broken, just

bruised. She hoped. She couldn't be hurt, not with her dad needing her, and Meg needing her.

Her eyes watered again, this time not from pain. And walking toward her was the most magnificent woman Bailey had ever seen. Willow Michaels, taller and more beautiful in person.

And with a smile that had to be genuine. Now why didn't that make Bailey like her? Why did it add depth to the stab of jealousy?

Because nice women were hard to resent. Because it was only on Monday that Cody had said cowboys wanted love and forever, too. And Willow looked like the type of woman who would make a man think about forever.

"Bailey Cross?" Willow's voice was husky and oddly toned.

Bailey hobbled across the arena, still leading the traumatized horse. She nodded in answer to Willow's question.

"Yes, I'm Bailey. You must be Willow."

Willow's hand went to her ear, just a flick and then she smiled again. "I am. Cody asked me to pick up a bull."

Bailey shifted her gaze in the direction of the bull. "There he is—the troublemaker."

"I'm sorry?"

"The bull, that's him."

Willow touched her arm. "I'm sorry, you'll have to look at me when you speak. The wind is carrying your words, and I can't hear you."

Bailey turned and Willow slid her hair back, allowing a small peek at the hearing aid hidden by the long tresses of blond. With that knowledge, Bailey suddenly didn't ache to be rid of Willow Michaels. She hadn't expected that, not when her first reaction had been jealousy. Jealous because Willow had a truck that didn't look like it was more scrap metal than anything else, and jealous because Willow smiled like smiling was easy.

"Of course, I'll speak up." Bailey added a smile of her own. "Would you like a glass of iced tea before we load the bull?"

"That would be lovely." Willow didn't talk like someone who had grown up in the country, or around farm animals. She sounded like someone used to tea served in china cups, not in plastic tumblers with ice.

Meg circled them, staring openly at the tall blond who towered over her mother. She took hold of Willow's hand and Willow leaned toward her.

"Do you know my dad?"

"I do know your dad. He's a friend."

The oddly unsettling pinch of jealousy returned, but Bailey swept it away, reminding herself that Willow was kind and obviously had a story. A woman as elegant as Willow, one who hauled bulls around the country, had to have a story.

"He likes my mom." Meg smiled sweetly, sashaying away before Bailey could get hold of her.

"I'm sorry, this is all new to her." Bailey hurried to explain. "She and Cody just met."

"I know—he told me." Willow looked down at Bailey's foot. "Are you okay?"

Okay? Did she mean okay with the fact that Cody had shared their story with this woman. She couldn't answer that because she didn't think she was okay. But Willow pointed to her foot, clearing up the misunderstanding.

"The buckskin shied and stepped on me. It's just a bruise." It couldn't be more than that, because working tomorrow wasn't optional.

And from there her thoughts spiraled to stacks of bills and repeated calls from the mortgage company. Her words for Cody came back to haunt her, that God wouldn't give them more than they could handle.

She hoped God knew she was holding tight to Him, and to faith.

As they walked through the back door of the house, greeted by still air and heat, Bailey's gaze traveled to her dad. He was at the table with a notebook and a calculator.

"Dad, I'll do that." Bailey covered his hand to stop him.

"I have to do something." He smiled up at her, his eyes less focused today and his skin papery and gray. His attention shifted to Willow. "Willow Michaels, nice to meet you."

Willow extended her hand to Jerry. "Nice to meet you, too."

Bailey poured three glasses of tea as Meg rummaged through the fridge for a juice box. The pink boots, a gift from an older woman at church, were getting small. How was she going to convince her daughter that some things had to be let go of?

She turned with the glasses of tea, and her heart sank as her gaze landed on her dad, remembering how he had looked just a few years earlier, before cancer. And she knew that her daughter wasn't the only one who had to learn that some things had to be let go of.

Bailey should have been an old pro by now. She had let go of her mom, Cody, and now her dad. She knew that she was going to have to let go of the farm.

After they drank their tea, Bailey and Willow walked back across the yard to the pen that had been the bull's home for the last week. Meg was in the house, sitting on her grandfather's lap watching the midday news.

"Life is never easy." Willow spoke as they neared the bull, the words so soft that Bailey had to strain to hear.

She wondered what in Willow's life had been difficult and then chastised herself for that thought. A beautiful face didn't guarantee that everything would be perfect.

"No, it isn't always easy." Bailey stopped at the gate to the pen. "Sometimes it is downright difficult."

Willow touched Bailey's shoulder. "Surviving makes our faith strong."

"You're very kind, Willow." Bailey thought she could even be friends with the other woman. "No wonder Cody thinks so much of you."

"He's just a friend." Willow smiled as she turned to walk away. "I'll back the trailer over here."

Bailey wanted to call out to Willow's retreating back that it didn't matter what Cody was to her. Really it didn't. After all, Bailey was used to letting go.

Cody shot through the air like a circus clown being ejected from a cannon. But he knew that the only net that would catch him was a hard dirt-packed arena floor, and no time to prepare for contact. On impact the thud of the ground knocked the air from his body and his head slammed backward.

And then darkness until the medic shouted his name.

"Cody, do you know where you are?" Dr. Charlotte Gaines, her black hair in a braid, spoke sharply. Sometimes he wondered why she had this job.

"I know who I am, and I know you don't like bull riders."

The crowd laughed because his words carried through the speakers. Dr. Gaines was wired for sound. The audience and the TV viewers liked that little extra insight.

"Cody, tell me where you are."

"Illinois," he mumbled as he tried to sit up, against the restraining hands of the doctor and her medic. A bullfighter, one of the guys who had saved his hide more than once, was laughing and mumbling that even on the ground, Cody was hitting on Dr. Gorgeous. He sat up, several pairs of hands holding his arms. "Did I get a reride?"

The bull hadn't spun; good bulls always spin. Instead he had made a straight line across the arena like a horse heading for the barn. At least Cody had lasted eight seconds. He distinctly remembered hearing the buzzer before his flying-monkey act.

And he remembered thinking about Meg, and how he wanted to be there for her, not part-time, not injured, but forever. And just as he hit the ground, he thought about Bailey lecturing him for taking chances.

Dr. Gaines didn't answer his question about a reride; instead, she ordered the medics to get him back to the exam room so she could get a better look at him.

Jason was at the gate when Cody walked through. Cody grabbed his friend's arm. "Did I get a reride?"

"Yes, you got your reride." Jason grabbed Cody's bull rope. "I'll get it ready for you."

Cody started to nod, but his head ached and he was seeing double. He swayed and Jason caught hold of his arm. Cody backed away, slipping free from the restraining hand of his friend.

"I'm fine."

"Of course you are." Jason shook his head and pushed the bull rope back into Cody's hand. "But I don't think you'll be riding."

"I'll ride." Cody let the medic lead him back to the exam room. Dr. Charlotte Gaines, small but straight as a rod, marched ahead of them.

The exam room was a makeshift emergency room, with everything the good doctor needed to examine her many patients each weekend. Two other bull riders were stretched out on cots, both with ice packs on various joints. Another was sitting on a chair, his foot up on a table but his gaze on the beautiful doctor.

"Sit." Dr. Gaines pointed and Cody did as she commanded.

She examined him, her frown growing with each minute that passed.

"I'm going to be fine."

"This time, Cody, but what about next time? How many concussions do you think you can take before the damage is permanent?"

He shrugged, because he wasn't an idiot and he knew the answer. He also knew she expected a little bit of a fight from him.

"But riding the reride bull could be the difference between winning this event or not." Cody knew she didn't care, but he reminded her anyway.

"Cody, you only get one brain and yours has taken more blows than is good."

"Oh, Dr. G, you say that to all the guys."

A slim smile slid across her lips and she shook her head. He had no feelings for her, other than those of a friend, but he did like to tease her, especially when he managed to produce one of her rare smiles.

"Fine, ride. I know I can't talk you out of it."

She slipped her stethoscope down and backed away from him. For a moment it wasn't her face that he saw, but Bailey's and then Meg's. That had to be the concussion.

"Did you know I'm a dad? Her name is Meg."

Her eyes softened with that maternal glimmer. "You have a daughter?"

"I met her for the first time a few weeks ago."

And he wasn't going to crack his skull and let her down. His days of taking chances were over.

"Congratulations." Charlotte Gaines patted his shoulder, the way she did when she was trying to distance herself. He knew her well enough to know that about her.

"Thanks. Now, if you'll let me have my walking papers, I'll let them know that I'm not taking the reride. Doctor's orders."

Because he had a daughter and he didn't want to let her down. He didn't want to put one more burden on Bailey. With everything else going on, she didn't need to hear that he was in the hospital, or worse.

Bailey pulled her truck past the gas pump and parked in front of the only convenience store in Gibson. It was packed, of course; on Sundays it was one of the few places open. With breath held—as if that would help—she eased out of her truck to keep from banging her door against the shiny paint of the Lexus parked next to her.

As her feet hit the ground, a sharp jab shot up her heel and she was reminded of the incident with Bucky the buckskin. She had named him because Cody hadn't bothered to tell her what to call the poor animal. *Bucky* didn't take a lot of creativity, and it wasn't an "I'm attached to the animal" kind of name.

She hobbled into the store, her left shoe feeling a size smaller than it should. Being on her feet while she waited tables for the Sunday lunch crowd at the diner hadn't helped. The work she still had to do at home would make it worse.

At least Mary, one of the Golden Girls, was at the house with Bailey's dad and Meg. Pastor John had called a few days earlier and given her a list of volunteers that would be showing up this week. He had been right, again. Knowing someone was there to help had given her peace of mind.

Okay, at first it hadn't been peace of mind but instead a definite stubbornness and the remark that she could manage.

Pastor John had reminded her that Christians were to serve one another and that she should let them put that act into practice.

Bailey smiled at a few people she knew in the store and made her way to the aisle of snack foods. Nothing like a nutritious meal to give her the energy she needed. Somehow she didn't think it would give her a boost. She was going on five hours of very interrupted sleep and the knowledge that her dad was failing fast.

"Bailey Cross, how are you?"

She turned at the familiar greeting and smiled at Chad Gardner. "Fine, Chad. How is Kate?"

"Still pregnant." He grinned like the father of a first child should, but the smile quickly faded. "Bailey, your dad called me about listing the farm, or at least the majority of the acreage."

Her heart jolted and for a few seconds she had to close her eyes to adjust. The fluorescent-lit convenience store, with neighbors walking the aisles, wasn't the place for this conversation, or the place for her to fall apart.

She had just wanted a package of cheese crackers.

"I didn't know."

"That's why I wanted to talk to you." He moved her to the side as a few teenagers crowded through the aisle. "I thought you should be in on the decision."

Her dad had gone behind her back. With everything else, she didn't need that. She wasn't angry with him, just hurt. Hurt because he thought he needed to speak to Chad on his own. And hurt because she knew it had to be done.

"Thank you, Chad, I appreciate your telling me."

"I drew the papers up and I'll bring them out for the two of you to sign. Whenever is good for you, but you should understand that a property that size could take six months or longer."

He didn't have to explain what he meant by that. She could lose the farm before it could sell. She smiled, pretending that everything would be okay.

"It's okay, Chad, we'll be fine."

"I know you will." He patted her arm and walked away.

Bailey hobbled to the racks of snack crackers and beef jerky. The diner had been busy, and she hadn't taken time for lunch. Now her stomach was growling, and even crackers with fake cheese spread sounded good.

"You know, that isn't good for you."

Bailey jumped at the familiar voice whispering in her ear as she reached for the package of six crackers. She turned, surprised by Cody's presence a day earlier than she had expected. And if she was honest, she was surprised he had even come back.

Really surprised.

"What are you doing here?"

"I have a daughter here."

Of course, a daughter. But that didn't eliminate the way her mood shifted to hopefulness, like a friend had shown up just in time.

"I saw the fall you took." And her heart had plummeted, seeing him on the ground for the second time in a year, watching as the medical staff rushed to his aid. "Are you okay?"

"A headache, but nothing a week or two off won't cure."

It would be another hit on his lead in the point standings. She knew how much those points meant. It meant the difference between winning a world championship, or not.

"What's the plan now?"

"Do you mean for bull riding?"

She continued on to the cooler section and opened the door to get a bottle of water. Cody reached around her and grabbed two, and then he looped his arm through hers. She wanted to tell him she didn't need his support, but it felt too good to object.

Maybe she should remind him about small-town rumors and how easily they got started? People had already figured out that he was Meg's dad.

"I meant, what are your plans for the future? Bull riding, when you plan to leave, and when do you want to set up a schedule for seeing Meg." It wasn't easy to bring up that last part about Meg, but it had to be said.

"I'm not leaving yet. And I don't want to talk about schedules to see my daughter. That makes it sound like I'm a visitor in her life."

"Fine, we won't talk schedules, but we can't avoid the facts. You had a life before you came here, a life that included a career and friends, and obviously a place you considered home."

"And now I have a daughter and responsibility. I'm going to figure it all out."

"Fine. But in the meantime…"

"Pastor John said the gossip is fading and that I should stay where I am. He's making sure everyone knows that the wedding is off."

"Oh, very funny." She couldn't help but smile. "So, your plans then?"

"I guess I'm leaving that up to you. I can't see moving the RV for a month or two and then moving it back to Oklahoma after the finals. I'd rather leave it where it is."

"That's fine; you can leave it."

"Why are you limping?" His hand reached for her arm and he pulled her to a gentle stop.

"Your buckskin—" she refused to admit she named the horse "—got spooked and stepped on me yesterday."

"Did you go to the doctor?"

No time, no money and she knew she didn't need to. "No, it's only a bruise."

"I'll look at it when we get home. And to make it up to you, let me buy you lunch."

"Lunch would be nice. What do you have in mind?" It was that easy to take him up on his offer. "Of course, keep in mind that the diner is closed. That's why I'm buying crackers."

"Leave it to me."

"I'm frightened."

He led her to the front of the store and pointed at the warming tray of fried foods. "Anything you want, price is no object."

"Anything?"

He nodded and swept his arm in a grand gesture to display her choices. "Anything."

Bailey laughed until her eyes watered, maybe because it was funny or maybe because of the sudden wave of relief that she couldn't explain.

"You mean, I can have chicken strips, egg rolls, corn dogs and fries with Cajun seasoning? Or even a mini pizza, or those little tacos?"

Cody motioned for the cashier. "We need two orders of everything, because I am not a cheap date."

At the word *date,* Bailey lost her appetite.

Chapter Nine

How could he expect her to sit in one place, her foot up and packed in ice, while there was work to be done? Bailey fumed as she sat on the porch, the food from the convenience store on a plate and a glass of iced tea sitting on the table next to her.

From across the yard, Meg yelled. She had found the kittens that the mother cat had hidden. Meg didn't understand that hiding the babies was the way a mother protected her young.

"He's just trying to take care of you, sis." Her dad's voice was weak, and he hadn't touched a bite of the food on his plate.

"I know, Dad. But I can't let myself get used to him being here."

"I don't see why not."

"Because…" Because she didn't have a good reason. She smiled at her dad. "I'm stubborn, like my dad, and I don't like to depend on someone else."

Because Cody wouldn't stay. He couldn't. She knew that about him, that he had a hard time putting down roots. She knew now that it had something to do with his childhood.

What kind of child had he been? Had he been lonely and

unloved? Had he been the kind of little boy who stayed in trouble?

She smiled at her dad, hoping to ease his concerns. He didn't smile back; he just moved his food around the plate and then set it down on the table.

Cody came out of the barn, his casual swagger as familiar to her as the blue of the sky. He headed in their direction, smiling as he got closer.

"How's the foot?" He leaned against the rail of the porch, his arms crossed over his chest and his dark hair damp from perspiration.

"Cold."

He laughed and kneeled next to her, moving the ice and touching her heel with his hand. "I don't think it's broken."

"I don't, either. Remember, that's why I wasn't worried."

"It is swollen."

"I was on my feet all day."

His hand, warm with a firm touch, rested on her ankle, and she moved to dislodge it. He leaned back on his heels and then stood, as if he suddenly couldn't handle the close contact, either.

The chair next to hers creaked. Bailey shifted her attention to her dad as he tried to stand. Cody moved to Jerry's side and wrapped an arm around his waist to help him to his feet.

"I think I need to sleep." Jerry smiled down at Bailey, and she told herself she couldn't cry. For him she had to smile.

"Okay, Dad. Ring the bell if you need anything." Harder than anything was the fact that Cody was taking over, and taking care of everyone.

"I'll be right back. Don't move," he ordered as they managed to get through the screen door side by side, her father and the father of her child.

Bailey's emotions were more bruised than her heel. She didn't think a person could put an ice pack on her heart. She did move the ice pack from her foot and dropped it onto the porch. Blue had joined her, and the dog licked the condensation off the plastic bag.

The screen door creaked open and Cody joined her again. His accusing gaze landed on her foot and then drifted to the dog and the ice pack.

"That's going to help." He sat down in the vacated seat next to hers.

"Blue was hot." Bailey focused on Meg in the yard with the kittens.

"School starts soon."

"It does."

"I'd like to be there, with the two of you."

"I don't mind." She didn't, but she did. She would have to share Meg's first day of school. She would have to face the public with Cody as Meg's father.

"If you don't want me there…"

"You should be there." Because he deserved to take part in one of Meg's *firsts,* and because he'd done so much for them.

"Your dad says he has an appointment tomorrow." Cody stretched and put his feet next to hers on the footstool.

Bailey bit down on her bottom lip and pretended it didn't bother her. "He needs new pain meds. I'm going to take off part of the morning to take him up to his doctor."

"I can take him."

Bailey moved her feet, dropping them to the floor of the porch. "I should do it."

"I'm here and I don't mind."

Bailey sighed and then nodded. "If you would, that would help."

She wondered if he knew how hard it was for her to let him in, not just him but anyone. She'd been used to doing things on her own for a long time.

Cody pulled up close to the house with Meg in the back of the truck sleeping and Jerry staring blankly out the window, a wet streak tracing down his cheek. The appointment for a new pain medication had turned into more than either of them had expected. It wouldn't be easy to talk to Bailey about what they had learned from the doctor.

He hadn't told Meg what the doctor had said, but he'd seen the worry in the little girl's eyes. To make it better, he did the only thing he knew how to do. He'd taken her shopping while the doctor ran tests on Jerry.

She would start school tomorrow. Hard to believe she was really old enough for that. She certainly didn't seem big enough. Or maybe he had a hard time thinking about letting go of someone he had just found.

He would have to deal with that because this farm, this steadiness, wasn't his life. Sooner or later, like every other time, he would get restless. He would feel the pull of bull riding, even if it did seem to be waning right at the moment. He would feel the urge to travel, even if for now his wandering feet seemed pretty content.

No matter what, he would always be there for Meg. He wouldn't let her down. He sighed at that, not wanting to be a weekend and summer-vacation dad.

"Ready to get out?" Cody turned to Jerry, who nodded. "Okay, let me help you."

"I can do it myself. You get the June bug into the house." Jerry glanced over his shoulder at his granddaughter. "Hard to believe she starts kindergarten tomorrow."

"I was just thinking the same thing."

Cody got out of the truck and opened the back door, reaching in to pull Meg out. She whimpered and curled against him, her face damp with perspiration and probably slobber. He smiled as she buried her face into his shoulder.

Man, she felt good in his arms. She made him feel strong and able to do anything. She made him feel like the hero he definitely wasn't. But it sure made him want to be one.

He walked through the house with her, perspiring in the warm air and feeling pretty good about having purchased the window air units in the back of his truck. Four of them. That should put a chill on this old farmhouse.

And the other thing in the back of his truck was a swing set for Meg.

Meg curled into her bed and he tucked her stuffed animal into her arms. She blinked a few times, smiled and drifted back off to sleep.

"I love you, sweet pea." He touched her cheek and walked back to the living room, where Jerry was settling into his recliner with his oxygen.

The blinds over the windows were drawn to keep afternoon sun from baking the room, and the only light came drifting in from the kitchen window. Cody reached to turn on the lamp but Jerry's words stopped him.

"Not every day that a man finds out he has less than two weeks to make sure his life is in order." Jerry fumbled with the tube in his nose and closed his eyes. "I don't have too many regrets."

Cody did. That seemed to be the theme of the year.

"What can I do to help?" He sat on the armrest of the brown plaid sofa in the stifling heat of the living room. The ceiling fan barely circulated a breeze, and the TV remained quiet for once. "Other than put those air conditioners in?"

"Now that'll be real nice." Jerry reached for the TV remote but pulled his hand back. "There is something else you can do for me, Cody."

Cody waited, unsure of what would be asked and how he would handle the request. He knew it would be big. He knew, with the tightening of his insides, that the request would change his life.

"I'll help you in any way I can."

Jerry nodded. "I know you will. Cody, take care of my girls. There are plenty of people around here who will look out for them, but not many who can stand toe-to-toe with Bailey. She's headstrong and used to taking care of things."

"I know, but I don't know how much she'll let me do for her."

Jerry sucked in a few deep breaths before he continued.

"Don't let her get away with trying to do it all on her own. She needs you."

Cody moved from the arm of the sofa to the seat. He stared at the dark paneled wall and tried to think of ways to explain to Jerry that he was the last thing Bailey needed.

"I'm not the right person for that job. I look at you and what a good man you are, like you don't even have to think about the right thing to do. I don't know how to be the person who always makes the right choices. I'm struggling with even being a dad to Meg."

Jerry smiled and sort of laughed. "You aren't any different from me or any other dad that I know. We all struggle, hoping we're doing the right thing."

"It seems like I do the wrong thing a lot more than I do the right thing."

Jerry's eyes closed. "She needs you. If you bought the land, you'd have a place of your own and you could be here to watch Meg grow up."

"I'll be here for her."

Jerry drifted off as Cody sat on the couch wondering how in the world he was going to keep that promise but knowing he would have to.

After overhearing the conversation between her dad and Cody, Bailey walked off the porch mumbling to herself about her dad's interference and Cody making promises he wasn't going to keep. Promises she wouldn't hold him to. She didn't need a babysitter, or a cowboy in shining armor.

On her way to the barn she passed Cody's truck. In the back were four rectangular boxes and one long box. She stepped closer to read the labels and then she turned and stomped back to the house.

Cody was coming out the back door and he looked perfectly innocent. She knew better.

"What in the world is in the back of your truck?" She ignored his finger raised to his mouth. She wasn't being that loud. "It looks like you've been shopping."

"We stopped by Wal-Mart on our way home from the doctor's office. Meg needed new shoes." He took hold of her arm, and she let him lead her away from the house. "Bailey, we need to talk about your dad."

Not about what her dad had asked him. She knew that from the serious look on his face.

"What happened?"

She didn't want to have this conversation. The look on Cody's face, the softness in his eyes—she didn't want to hear. It was meant to be only a checkup today; that's why she hadn't gone. Her dad had needed new medications, and the doctor had wanted to see him first.

She should have gone. Guilt was tangling with dread like

barn cats fighting in the hayloft, twisting and turning in her stomach.

Cody's hand gripped her arm as if he was afraid she might fall. She was afraid, too. Her head was swimming and the only thing keeping her upright was the man standing in front of her.

"The doctor said it could be less than two weeks."

Air conditioners and swings were no longer important. Conversations about Cody taking care of her meant nothing. Useless anger wouldn't solve anything.

Bailey covered her eyes with her hand and waited for the world to right itself, but that wasn't going to happen, not this time, not yet. She knew that eventually she would recover; she would move forward and life would return to some semblance of normal. But she also knew that in a matter of weeks there would be a hole, a vacancy where her dad's presence should have been.

A hand touched her arm and she moved her hand from her eyes to look up at Cody. Were those tears shimmering in his eyes? She would have taken a closer look, but he didn't give her a chance. His arms closed around her, and he pulled her close, holding her against his solid chest as sobs rolled through her body.

"I'll be here," Cody promised.

This time she didn't argue with him. She didn't have the strength to protest or to tell him she didn't expect him to stay forever. She wouldn't hold him to the promise he'd made to her dad.

Cody's cheek rested on the top of her head, and Bailey couldn't convince herself to pull free from his arms. Not yet. She wanted to melt into him, to soak up his strength and pretend for a few minutes that he was going to stay forever.

"Mom." Meg's happy shout ended the moment.

Bailey pulled back, wiping her eyes with the back of her hand and then lifting the neckline of her shirt to wipe away the mascara that would have smeared. Cody blocked Meg's view for those few seconds.

"Hey, kiddo, did you have a good day?" She leaned to hug her daughter, the gesture bringing to light the reason for her daughter's happy smile. "Are those new boots?"

Meg did a dance and then raised one foot for Bailey to see the brown boots with white flowers going up the outside of each. The boots were leather, expertly tooled and hadn't come from a discount store.

"Dad bought them for me because my pink ones were getting too small."

Bailey wanted to cry all over again. She wanted to cry because Meg was learning to let go, and because Cody had been able to do what Bailey had wanted to do. And he hadn't even had to think about it. He didn't have to count one penny or make one end meet another.

"And he said we could have the buckskin, that it can be my horse someday 'cause Dad bought it."

Cody groaned. At least he had the sense to do that.

Bailey didn't sigh, but she wanted to. She didn't tell her daughter that she couldn't have the boots, the swing set or the horse. She wouldn't punish Meg. Instead she gave Cody a look that if he didn't understand it, he'd better learn the language.

"That's wonderful, Meg." Bailey kissed her daughter on the top of the head. "Why don't you run inside and get yourself a Popsicle? I'm going to go feed the cows."

"I'll help you." Cody followed as she headed toward the barn.

"You've helped enough."

"Bailey, could you give me a chance to explain?"

Bailey grabbed the barn doors and jerked to swing them open; the door didn't budge. Cody moved the latch that he had hung and pulled. The door swung with ease.

"Everything is easy for you, isn't it, Cody? Being the hero is easy. Giving my daughter what I can't is easy. And walking away is easy."

Somewhere deep inside she knew she wasn't being reasonable. She didn't need the look from Cody to tell her that, or her own conscience to goad her into backing down. She knew, but she hurt so much she couldn't stop herself from saying the words.

"Will the gifts make you feel better when you leave? Like the dozen roses you sent me the day you left Wyoming? Like that would undo everything and make it okay. The only thing the gifts undo is the guilt you feel."

"I didn't buy Meg these gifts to make myself feel better." He followed her into the barn, just a step behind, and she could tell from his movements that he was angry.

She spun around, not wanting her back to him. "So, this isn't about what makes you feel better?"

He ran both hands through his hair and shook his head, his fingers still buried in the hair at the back of his head.

"I don't know, maybe it is." He looked away, giving her a clear view of his clenching jaw. "I haven't been here, Bailey. I've missed out on a lot, and I have a lot to make up for. You've had her the whole time. Give me a break if I haven't completely passed Parenting 101."

Give him a break. Forgive him. Admit that the anger with Cody was just easier than dealing with what he had told her about her dad. Bailey unlatched the feed-room door, pulling the string to switch on the light as she stepped into the dark. Mice scurried to hide and the room smelled like molasses and leather.

She breathed in a moment, comforting herself with something familiar and unchanging.

"Bailey, I missed out on everything. I missed out on Meg's first smile, her first tooth and her first birthday."

"Yes, but now you're the hero, giving her everything that I've never been able to give her. You're making me feel like the one who has let her down."

"I didn't mean to make you feel that way."

"No, I know you didn't. But you have to understand how much I've wanted to give her and how hard it has been to raise her on my own. I had Dad, and he did his best. But the last few years have really been hard on us."

"I can't undo what I didn't know about."

More guilt. Her own this time. He didn't have a monopoly on that emotion.

"Neither of us can undo what has happened." She scooped grain into a bucket and he grabbed the handle. "We just have to try and be grown-ups from this point on."

"Can she keep the gifts I've given her, or do you want me to take them back?"

Bailey allowed herself to smile at that. "No, she can keep them. I really like the buckskin."

Cody walked out of the feed room with the bucket of grain. When they walked into the sunlit corral where the cows had come up to be fed, he stopped. Bailey came to a halt next to him, wondering what had happened. She looked at the black angus cows. They were all there, and all looked healthy.

"What?"

"Bailey, you act like it is all worked out—everyone is happy. I'm not. Sometimes I'm so mad at you, I want to shake you. Sometimes I want to leave and not look back." He shook his head. "I'm going to have to take a break and attend an AA meeting in Springfield. I'm not as able to handle this on my own as I thought."

He set the bucket down and walked away. She started to say something to stop him, but he raised a hand and kept going. As Bailey poured grain into the feed trough for the cows, she heard his truck start and then heard the crunch of gravel on the drive as he left.

Each time he left and then came back, it was as if he proved something to her. She wondered what it would feel like if he didn't come back.

And then her thoughts took a different turn as a solid truth sank in. Soon she would know how it felt for her dad to leave and not come back.

All of the anger melted. It hadn't really been about Cody, the past or his gifts to Meg. It all came down to her dad and not knowing how to deal with losing him.

Tears streaked down her face, wetting her lips with their saltiness as she broke apart a few flakes of hay for the cows and tossed it over the fence. Everyday chores, as if nothing was wrong. Her body shook as the reality of the doctor's forecast for her dad really hit home.

When she walked into the house, Jerry was waiting at the kitchen table for his afternoon meds. Meg was in the yard with Blue, throwing a ball for the dog who had no limits on her energy or capacity to play.

"Sis, your eyes are red." Her dad reached out and Bailey took hold of his hand. She swallowed a lump and then leaned down to hug him.

"I don't want to do this." She whispered into his thinning gray hair. "I don't want to talk about losing you."

"Life has seasons, Bailey—we both know that. This is my season to die and yours to mourn. But there will be a new season for us both. Yours is going to be full of hope and promise here, and mine is going to be in Glory."

He was still teaching her lessons on life. Bailey cried and his hand held her back, trembling as he pulled her close.

"I thought there would be another answer, Dad. I really thought God would answer my prayers."

"He's giving us peace to get through this." He pulled his hand back and Bailey sat down in the seat next to his. "He answered by bringing Cody, whether you see it as an answer or not."

"But I don't want to lose you."

His skin was gray and his mouth tight. Bailey knew he was in pain. He reached and covered her hand with his. "Let me go, Bailey. Don't pray to keep me here—pray for God to do His will."

And face the world without him in it? She wanted to tell him she couldn't do that, but she knew she could. She knew that her tears would be for her own loss, but that her dad would no longer be suffering. She'd been given time to adjust, and she knew she could make it.

She smiled to ease his fears for her. "We'll make it, Dad."

"I know you will. You're stronger than you think, Bailey."

She didn't feel strong.

Cody pulled his truck up to the RV, switched off the engine and then just sat. It was dark and the only light on in the house was the kitchen light. Blue was sleeping under the picnic table next to his RV. He'd seen her there when he pulled up, her eyes glowing red in the headlights of his truck. He had seen her tail thump a greeting, recognizing him as someone who belonged there.

Tonight he'd sat in a meeting with twenty other people who

could admit they were tempted to drink. The group had consisted of a banker, a salesman, a housewife, a business owner, a doctor and a construction worker. Those were the ones he remembered. He hadn't felt so out of place, thinking he had to be the lowest of the low. All types of people struggled and made mistakes.

On the drive back to Gibson, he had prayed for help, for strength and for answers. He didn't know where to go from here. Back to Oklahoma, back on tour with the gold buckle in mind, or should he stay in Gibson?

He'd made Jerry Cross a promise to take care of things. He didn't really know how to do that or how far the promise went. He knew how to ride bulls. He had a degree in marketing and business. He knew how to live a temporary life without roots. He'd seen what roots could do to something. Roots could wrap around the wrong thing and strangle the life out of it.

But sometimes roots just dug down and gave life.

He closed his eyes, wondering if staying in Gibson would be good roots or bad. So far it felt good, but he also felt bruised. He felt like that vine that Jesus had talked about, being clipped and pruned. So the roots would go deeper and be stronger.

He opened his eyes and saw the shadow of Bailey as she walked across the kitchen. At one time he had wanted her to be his roots, what kept him strong. But she hadn't been. She'd just been the person who made him want to be strong. Fear had been the dominate emotion in Wyoming. Fear that he'd let her down. Fear that if he didn't get away, she would hold him in one place.

He felt it again, that fear of not being the one who could be strong for her. What if he slipped and fell off the wagon? Would four or five more months of sobriety, making it to that one-year anniversary, really prove anything?

Crossing the lawn a few minutes later, he hesitated, almost turning away from the house. Blue barked and Bailey walked out the back door. That took it out of his hands.

"Look what the cat dragged in." She smiled in the dark shadows of the porch, her hair in a ponytail with wisps of blond coming loose to frame her face.

"I saw that you were still up. I wanted to make a last-ditch attempt at apologizing."

"No, I should apologize." She joined him in the front yard. "I was hurt because you make it all seem so easy. You can give Meg what I can't. And you gave my dad the peace of mind I couldn't."

She had lost him. "What do you mean by that?"

"I heard you tell him you'd take care of us."

"What was I supposed to do? Did you want me to tell him that I'm walking and I'm not about to stay here and make sure you're okay?"

"I don't want you to lie to him. And I don't want you to think that I need you to take care of me. I'm letting you out of your promise."

"Okay, fine." He started to turn but she caught hold of his arm. Her hand was soft and tentative, like in his dreams.

"Cody, I didn't come out here to fight. I came because I have something for you."

"What?"

"Come inside—it's in the kitchen."

He followed her into the house, which was still too warm. Tomorrow he would get those air conditioners installed and put up the swing set for Meg. He had a long list of things that he would get done, tomorrow.

Tonight Bailey had a gift for him. She pointed to a photo album and a videotape on the table. "Those are for you."

He looked at her and then picked up the photo album. Page one, Bailey pregnant. The young woman in the picture smiled but shame flickered in her dark eyes. She looked alone.

He hadn't been there for her. And now her dad expected him to be the one who wouldn't let her down. His track record wasn't very good.

"You were beautiful." He sat down at the table, and she sat down across from him. She was still beautiful. Her skin was sun-kissed and makeup-free. Her eyes were so warm he thought he'd melt if she looked into his heart.

She made him want to be the man of her dreams, the man she had assumed he was all those years ago. He had made sure she knew better because he hadn't wanted her to count on him. He had counted on his dad; look how that had turned out.

"It was hard." Bailey leaned across the table to study the pictures he was looking at, bringing the fresh herbal scent of her shampoo with her. "I loved that baby growing inside me and I struggled with shame and guilt."

"And my presence here brought that all back."

"In a way. People had forgotten, but you made them remember. You're Meg's dad and we're not married."

He flipped the page to study the pictures because he couldn't look at Bailey. Instead he looked at his daughter's first day of life. She was pink and wrinkled, with a bow in her one strand of hair. She was beautiful. He closed his eyes as it really hit home what he'd missed out on and what he couldn't get back. Through pictures he took a five-year trip, seeing the *firsts* in Meg's life.

"This is why I buy her gifts." He finally looked up. Bailey was watching him. "Because it's all I can give her. You gave her everything else, Bailey. You gave her the things that really matter. You gave her life. You gave her comfort and love. You walked the floors with her when she couldn't sleep."

"Then maybe we're even." Bailey shrugged as she stood up. "Do you want a glass of ice water?"

"No thanks. If you don't care, I'd like to take these back to the RV and spend some time looking at them."

"Of course you can. I went through all of my other photo albums and made that one for you. It's yours to keep and to take with you."

Her unspoken words hit home. When he left, he would have something to take, something to help him remember his daughter. It made him feel like the loser on a game show, walking away with the consolation prize.

"Thank you." He pushed the screen door open, and she followed him out.

"Tomorrow is Meg's first day of school. I wanted to make sure you're planning to go with us."

The reminder caught him off guard. He stopped at the top step, Blue at his side and Bailey standing at the door. She was offering to make him a part of one of the *firsts* in his daughter's life.

"I would really like to be there." He walked off the porch. Standing in the yard, he turned to face her. "It means a lot to me, that you're willing to let me share in her life."

"I want you to stay in her life, Cody. She needs you there." She walked down the steps. "I know that you have to leave soon, but please don't be the dad who shows up just to buy gifts."

Don't be his own father. She didn't know about his dad.

"Bailey, I love my daughter and I'm going to be a real part of her life. I'm not going to buy her gifts to make up for not being here."

She shook her head and he knew that she was remembering the roses she got after he left the first time. He had given her a gift to make up for not being there. Standing there in the dark with Bailey a silhouette in the light from the porch, he remembered another summer night and the trust she'd given him.

"I'm sorry." He didn't know what else to say but he had to say more. "I'm sorry for walking away. I'm sorry for everything. Most of all, I'm sorry that you don't trust me."

"I'm trying."

He nodded, but he didn't have more words; he only knew that leftover feelings were emerging and Bailey stood in front of him, trying to trust. Tentative, he took a step closer, breathing in her clean scent and wondering how this one woman had the ability to undo everything he thought about himself.

When she reached up and touched his cheek, he closed his eyes and remembered how it felt to want to keep her in his life. He opened his eyes and looked for answers in hers. Leaning in, he looked for something more as he covered her mouth with his.

The kiss lasted moments, but it felt like a lifetime. And when she stepped away, he didn't know how to let her go.

"The roses were a bad idea, Bailey."

She pulled away, smiling. "Yes, the roses were a bad idea. Don't forget, tomorrow morning we take Meg to school."

She left him standing alone in the yard, clouds covering the moon and dampness in the air promising rain. He turned toward his RV, carrying the gifts she had given him. The photo album and the videotape weren't parting gifts. They felt more like an invitation for him to be a real part of his daughter's life.

And he wanted to believe the invitation extended to Bailey's life.

Chapter Ten

"Okay, smile one more time real big." Camera poised, Bailey caught another *first* for the photo album. Meg in one of her new outfits—a denim skirt, peasant blouse and the boots that Cody bought—standing next to her grandfather. It was her first day of school.

It was the first time a *first* included a picture of Cody and Meg together. It was the first time a *first* had been shared. Bailey felt as if she was on a teeter-totter, going up and down. Jealousy mingled with selfishness and some other feeling, something that resembled expectancy. A feeling of things to come. She couldn't handle that thought, not right now.

The entire morning had been a combination of rolling emotions and giggles from the little girl who couldn't believe she was finally going to school. The rolling emotions were Bailey's because she couldn't believe her daughter was big enough to go off by herself and be gone all day.

"Shouldn't you all be going?" Jerry nodded in the direction of the clock on the fireplace mantle. "Nearly eight now."

"Yes, we should go." But Bailey didn't want to. Her little

girl was standing in front of her, one tooth missing and a smile that said life was better than a carnival. And the only thing Bailey could think of was that little baby she'd brought home from the hospital nearly six years ago.

That day she had been alone. Today Cody stood in the living room, not really a part of her life, and yet…

He was here. And he wasn't a kid anymore with a smile that said life was just for fun, without responsibility. This Cody had a smile that said he'd learned a lot in the last six years. He had laugh lines around his eyes and a hint of gray in his dark hair.

Smiling, he took the camera from Bailey's hand and set it down on the table. "Can't have her late on the first day."

Meg hugged her grandfather and then raced to the kitchen for her new backpack and lunch box. Both were pink with her favorite cartoon character on the front. Bailey followed slowly, not really giving into the excitement that everyone else seemed to feel.

Ten minutes later they pulled into the school parking lot with all of the other parents bringing their kids for the first day.

They looked like a family. A father, mother and daughter.

As they walked down the sidewalk with Meg in the middle holding each of their hands, Bailey tried to pretend the illusion was real. For Meg's sake.

The illusion was shattered as they entered the building and walked down the hall to Gladys Parker's kindergarten class.

Half the town of Gibson was at school that morning, and most of them were looking at Bailey, Cody and Meg. Bailey could imagine what they were thinking. Some knew who Cody was; others were putting it all together or making up some new rumor. Bailey didn't have to hear the words.

She knew all about curiosity. People needed something to talk about at supper because the same old gossip could get as stale as the bread at the convenience store. Bailey wished they'd find something other than her life. Maybe they could talk about how pretty Myrtle Lewis's flowers looked, or the color of the new fire truck.

Maybe they could discuss how a rooster could possibly get arrested for crowing and disturbing the peace. That little incident had happened a month ago, and it had to be more interesting than what was going on at the Cross farm.

Meg's steps had slowed and Bailey was able to concentrate on something other than the heat crawling up her neck and settling in her cheeks. Her daughter and the first day of school definitely took precedence over gossip.

When they reached the door of the kindergarten class, Bailey stopped, ignoring Cody's questioning looks. The minute they stepped over the threshold, a new phase of life started for Meg, and for herself.

"Are you ready for this?" She pulled Meg close and hugged her again, remembering the verses her dad had shared the other day about life's seasons.

It was Meg's time to grow and to take this new step. And Bailey's time to let go. And she could do that. In a minute, after she held her daughter tightly and said a quick prayer over her that this day would be a good one.

"Bailey Cross, wasn't it just yesterday that I had you in this class?" Gladys Parker stood in the doorway, looking not much older than she had twentysomething years ago. "You were here my first year. My goodness, where did the time go?"

Bailey stood, pretending her throat wasn't tight and tears weren't burning her eyes. She could do this. She could smile and turn her daughter over to Mrs. Parker.

"I haven't lost one yet, Bailey." The teacher, hair still brown and only a few wrinkles around her eyes to show the passing of time, took Meg's hand, and Meg wasn't at all hesitant. She skipped into the room, waving goodbye as she ran to join the kids she already knew.

"Have a good day, Meg." But Meg wasn't paying attention. Bailey choked back a sob and the feeling that she was no longer needed. Of course Meg needed her.

"See you at three, Bailey." Mrs. Parker patted her arm and walked away, as if this happened every day. Bailey guessed it probably did. Anxious mothers, happy children taking new steps and teachers who had been through the process dozens of times.

"That was too easy." Bailey turned away from the room, trying not to think about how easy it was to have Cody's arm around her waist, walking her out of the school.

"Easy for Meg to let go, not so easy for her parents." Cody spoke in a voice almost as choked up as her own.

Parents, plural. Another *first*.

A few minutes later Cody stopped in front of the Hash-It-Out.

"Do you want me to pick you up this afternoon?"

Bailey reached for the door handle. "Lacey said she would take me to get Meg and bring me home."

"Good, then I'm going to work on your truck and get a few things done around the house."

They stared at each other, and Bailey was the first to move, to break the moment that had become too strange. Or maybe he hadn't felt it, felt that thread that connected them like they were a couple, like this mattered and meant something.

She pushed the door open and mumbled goodbye as she hopped to the pavement and hurried toward the front door of the diner, aware of the diesel rumble of Cody's truck as it rolled slowly away.

It all felt like someone else's life. Bailey knew it wouldn't last, this feeling of things coming together and being right. As she walked through the front door of the diner, the bell clanged and a few of the regulars—farmers in work clothes and worn leather boots—turned to smile. Lacey waved from the waitress station.

How could it feel like every other day when it wasn't? Today was Meg's first day of school, and yesterday she had learned that she would have her dad only for a few more days.

A farmer with a neighboring piece of land raised his coffee cup as she walked past. Bailey nodded and headed for the waitress station and a pot of coffee.

"First day of school. How exciting is that?" Lacey already had the coffee pot.

"Exciting? No, more like traumatic."

Lacey paused to talk. The farmer called out to her, but she waved him off and shook her head. "Didn't Meg want to go to school?"

Bailey laughed at her friend's genuine concern. "Meg wasn't the one traumatized, I was."

"I can see how it would be traumatic, having to go through all of that and then being dropped off at the front door by a gorgeous man."

"He's only here temporarily."

"He only stopped to talk. How long ago?"

Bailey took the coffee pot from Lacey. "Mr. Donaldson wants his coffee."

"Avoidance won't make it go away, Bay."

"Will it make you go away?"

Bailey's truck was a lost cause. Or at least it was by Cody's definition. He hadn't ever been much of a mechanic. He could do the basics, but this looked like an engine problem. And he knew that Bailey didn't have the money to have it rebuilt or replaced.

He could have it done for her. How well would that go over?

He dropped his tools into the toolbox and closed the lid. The mailman was pulling away from the mailbox, and Blue was barking at the side of the road. He would get the mail, fix Jerry some lunch and find something else to repair.

Maybe the swing set. He'd already put in the air conditioners. He could hear the hum and he knew the house would be cooling off.

As he walked down the drive to get the mail, Blue hurried to reach him. She bounced around, her bobbed tail wagging and her tongue lolling out one side of her mouth. Late summer heat beat down on Cody's head; obviously the dog didn't feel it.

"You crazy dog." He patted her head and she bounded ahead of him.

He grabbed the pile of envelopes out of the mailbox and headed back to the house. His mouth was dry and his mind had settled on those air conditioners and a glass of iced tea. And he'd try to think of something tempting for lunch. Maybe he could get Jerry to eat.

Probably not.

He entered the house through the back door. The kitchen was already a good ten degrees cooler than it had been. The lights were off and the only noise, other than the hum of the AC units, was the sound of the news on the TV in the living room. He poured himself a glass of tea and checked the contents of the fridge.

"That you, Cody?"

"It's me."

Cody walked into the living room and sat down on the sofa, the mail still in his hands. It wasn't his mail and wasn't his business. He glanced up, meeting the unfocused gaze of a man who had asked him to take care of things. No, more than things—he wanted Cody to take care of Bailey and Meg.

"What's wrong?"

"Another letter from the mortgage company." Cody held it out but Jerry shook his head.

"You read it."

"It isn't my business, Jerry. I don't think Bailey would want me to step this far into her life."

"I'm asking."

Cody pulled out his pocketknife and opened it, sliding the blade through the top of the envelope. He took the letter out, silently reading over it and then reading it to himself one last time. He sat back, trying to think of his next move.

"It's a foreclosure notice, isn't it?" Jerry closed his eyes as a tear slid down his cheek. "I never should have gotten that line of credit on this place. I just didn't know how to pay the medical bills."

"You did what you had to, Jerry. There's no shame in that." Cody looked over the letter again as he took a long drink of iced tea. "It's a final notice stating the amount you need to bring the loan back into good standing. I could pay this for you."

"And then we'd still have those payments to make. I appreciate the offer, Cody, but it would only be a temporary fix." Jerry closed his eyes and didn't open them when he continued. "The payment went up last year. We handled it until then."

"Then I'll buy the land. I've wanted a place of my own."

"I thought you were worried about making her mad."

"I want you to know she's taken care of. This is something

I can do." Because he couldn't promise to be in Bailey's life and he was positive that's what Jerry really wanted.

"Do you know what it's listed for?" Jerry's voice was getting weaker.

"I do, and I'm willing to pay it all. We'll call Chad and I'll cut you a check today. We can get the closing done, we can notify the mortgage company and it will be taken care of. Bailey will have enough left over to set up the horse farm she's wanted, and she won't have to worry."

"It isn't about the money, Cody."

Lost, Cody leaned forward, not sure what he was meant to take away from Jerry's statement. Pain medication could do that to people, make them groggy and unable to connect sentences or thoughts.

"I'm sorry, Jerry, I don't understand."

Jerry didn't answer right away. They sat in silence, Jerry's eyes closed, and Cody waiting.

"Jerry?"

"I want more for my daughter than your money. She needs more. Meg needs more."

Cody got it.

"I know, Jerry, and I'm doing my best. I'm still learning." He scooted to the edge of the couch. "I didn't have a dad like you, someone who showed me the right way."

"You have a God who will, so stop looking for excuses."

Excuses? He could have argued; instead he let the words sink in, and he wondered if that was what his parents had become for him. They'd made mistakes so they were to blame for every wrong decision he made? He couldn't let that be his life. Not anymore. He had to make decisions based on what he believed was the right thing to do.

Bailey and Meg were a big factor in that.

Jerry fell asleep and Cody went to the kitchen to call the real-estate agent. His mind continued to whirl after the call and while he was sitting in the shade trying to put together his first swing set.

Swing sets, he realized, needed an assembly book for dummies. There were a few too many screws, there were too few parts, and nothing really seemed to match up. The directions in the box weren't written in English.

From time to time his gaze traveled to the hundred-thirty acres he'd agreed to buy. His land. He had worked for it, saved for it, and now he'd have it. At what cost? Surely more than the actual price he was paying.

Jerry was right. It wasn't all about the money. And it could no longer be about what Cody's own father had done wrong. It had to be about what he was going to do right.

At the end of the drive, right under the oak tree, was the biggest swing set Bailey had ever seen. From the backseat of Lacey's car, Meg was shouting and breathless from excitement. Her first day of school, and now this. Could life for a five-year-old get any better?

Bailey turned and smiled at her daughter. She should tell her to calm down, but it wouldn't do any good. Besides that, a swing set was a big deal to a little girl. Bailey remembered her own and how she had sat on the ground and watched her dad put it together.

Bailey's dad had been her hero. Looking at Meg, her blue eyes focused on Cody as if he could do no wrong, Bailey knew that a part of her daughter's heart now belonged to Cody.

She was okay with that. Really she was. Even if it did hurt a little. It felt worse than when she was a kid and her dad's cattle dog had licked off the best bite of her candy bar, which meant giving the greedy thing the entire treat.

"Can I swing now? Please, Mom?" The car had stopped and Meg was hurrying to unbuckle. "I don't have to have a snack."

Cody was attaching the slide, and the swings were already in place. He waved and smiled. Bailey smiled as Lacey chuckled. That earned her friend a look.

"But I brought you cheese fries from the diner." Bailey glanced in the backseat at her daughter. Meg's seat belt was off and she was reaching for the door handle.

"I can have cheese fries anytime."

"Okay, you can swing. But don't leave the yard." Bailey barely got the words out, and Meg was out of the car and running across the lawn.

"Sweet." Lacey smiled and said the word with a soft longing. "You've got something good going on here, Bailey. I know I've teased you a lot, but this is good."

"This is temporary, and I don't want Meg to be hurt."

"He isn't going to walk out of her life."

"Yeah, I know." She glanced at Lacey and saw understanding. "Want to come in?"

"Nope, I have a lot of yard work to catch up on. Call me if you need anything."

Bailey nodded and got out of the car. Warm summer air and the scent of drying grass greeted her. Cody smiled in her direction, a pleased look on his face. He was the hero. She could let him have his moment.

She walked across the yard to where Cody stood. Meg was already swinging, her legs kicking to push the swing higher.

"I need iced tea and I have to check on Dad. Do you want anything, or are you going to stay out here?"

"I'll come in with you."

She didn't expect that, or the tight expression on his face as if something was wrong. "For a man who made a little girl's day, you look pretty serious."

He followed her up the steps to the porch and reached ahead of her to open the door. "We really need to talk."

"Hey, you put the AC units in. I bet you're my dad's hero, too."

"In more ways than one," he mumbled, making her think she might have misunderstood.

"What does that mean?" Bailey flipped on a light and opened the refrigerator door. "Get a couple of glasses down."

She turned with the pitcher of tea and saw a pile of papers on the table. Cody's gaze shifted away from her and the papers. He opened a cabinet and pulled out the glasses while she set the pitcher down and walked to the table.

"What is this?"

"Bailey, we had to do something."

Her chest ached and her hands trembled as she sifted through the paperwork. "No, Cody, you can't do this. A swing for a little girl is one thing, but this is my family farm."

"Bailey, we can't let them auction it off on the courthouse steps. You can't lose a farm that has been in your family for almost a hundred years."

"But I did lose it, didn't I? Now it's your farm."

"It isn't going to be sold to a developer who will divide it into five-acre parcels. And that is exactly who was hovering over it. Chad had received three calls already."

Bailey dropped onto a chair and buried her face in her hands. She couldn't deal with this. A part of her mind knew that it had to happen and that Cody had saved the land she loved so much. And part of her saw him as the person who could do everything she couldn't.

Maybe that was okay. Maybe it was good, to know that he had it and it wouldn't be lost.

His hand was on her shoulder, warm and strong. She didn't want to feel anything for a minute, not comforted, or relieved, or like the rug was about to be jerked out from under her. And she felt all of those things.

She wanted to thank God for providing an answer. And she wanted to ask Him why it had to be this answer.

"I'm sorry." Cody moved his hand and stepped away from her. "I wish I could do the right thing for once."

"Cody, you did the right thing. I'll deal with this."

"Is this about your pride? Do you realize how ridiculous that is? What is more important, you being in control or your dad having peace of mind?"

"Dad, of course. And this farm, knowing it will be here and that it won't be divided." She could say the words and even know that the words were the truth.

"Then why don't you relax and realize what this does for your life. You don't have to worry about how to make ends meet, they've been met and for a good long while."

Air-conditioning, her daughter on a swing set in the backyard and now a farm that was out of debt. She had the house and twenty-five acres to build a dream.

And Cody standing in her kitchen, confident that he had fixed everything. Except her truck. He hadn't been able to fix the beast.

"Bailey, it's done, so let it be."

He had taken care of them, just like he promised her dad. And it hit her just like that. His hands were clean. He'd done what her dad had asked, and now when he left, he wouldn't have a guilty conscience. He wouldn't even have to send her roses.

The thought of him walking away hurt more than anything. But she would let it be about the land because that was easier to deal with.

"Fine, it's done. Now why don't you go work on fixing your own life and leave mine alone for a while?"

Chapter Eleven

Fix his own life. Cody replayed Bailey's words over and over in the next few days. He had fixed fences, fixed her finances and made his daughter happy. In a way, he had been fixing his life. He'd at least been making himself feel better about things he'd done.

Maybe he'd just been fooling himself. The real fixing of his life had to do with the foundation: his parents. He hadn't talked to his mother in three years. She was living in Paris with her new husband. He had tried calling, but she was away for the next month. That was typical when he called.

His dad was in California. Cody opened his cell phone and dialed a number he hadn't dialed in a long time. When his dad answered, it took him a few seconds to adjust.

"Dad, it's Cody."

"Cody, I haven't heard from you in a while. What do you need?" Of course his dad would think it had to do with money or some other problem that needed to be solved.

That's what fathers did; they solved problems.

"I don't need anything. I wanted to call and touch base." He looked out the window at Bailey on the buckskin and Meg sitting on the grass with a black, orange and white kitten. She liked calico cats; so did he. "Dad, I have a daughter."

"You're married? Seems like that is something a father should know."

"I'm not married."

"Well, that explains why I haven't heard about this."

"She's five years old and I didn't know about her." As he said the words, he counted reasons his dad had for feeling ashamed. Maybe this call hadn't been a good idea. Maybe it had been the worst idea ever.

"Are you going to do the right thing?" Dalton Jacobs, neurosurgeon, *always* did the right thing.

Cody crushed down anger and resentment and searched for forgiveness, the real reason for this call. "I'm trying to do the right thing."

He was thirty years old and when he talked to his dad, he still felt like the seventeen-year-old kid who ran a car through the neighbor's fence. Back then doing the right thing had meant spending an afternoon repairing a fence.

"I'm glad to hear that. Listen, Cody, I have to go. Melinda is having a dinner party tonight, and I need to do something for her." Always for Melinda. "Next time you're in California, come by. I miss you."

Never those words before. Cody glanced out the window again, the tightness around his heart easing. "I'll be out there in a few months."

"Good. And, son, congratulations."

Cody hung up, but he felt better. He felt better knowing that he had talked to his dad, because a person never knew what tomorrow might bring. And he felt relieved because he had finally forgiven his dad for walking away.

He walked outside and across the yard to the corral, where Bailey was working the buckskin. She slid off and then re-mounted, leaning over the horse's neck to whisper to him. She loved the horse. And he felt a twinge of something sharp, like jealousy. Of a horse?

He watched as she worked the animal, first walking him around the arena, then a slow trot and then a controlled lope, with the horse leading with the right foot. It was easy to watch her ride. It was almost lyrical, woman and horse, fluid and one.

That jealousy thing stabbed at him again because she felt that oneness with a horse and yet she was barely talking to him.

Bailey slowed the horse to an easy walk and rode to the fence where he stood. Cody leaned on the top rail and waited. She slid to the ground with an easy grace and walked over to him. He remembered why he had been drawn to her in Wyoming.

Because she was the real deal. She was genuine and her smile felt like sunshine after a hard winter.

"I forgive you." She said it as if it was the natural progression of things, and he didn't quite know what she was talking about.

"Forgive me?"

She smiled. "The land. It isn't easy, being rescued. Especially when I've been working so hard to rescue us for the last few years. You made it seem like it was nothing. You made a call, wrote a check and tah-dah—problem solved."

"I didn't mean to do that to you." He reached for her hand and she gave it, her fingers lacing through his. "I called my dad."

"Okay."

Of course she didn't understand. He rarely shared his life with anyone. "I haven't talked to him in a while. I wanted him to know about Meg."

A range of emotions shifted across her face, like clouds

playing across the sky. "It sounds like you and your dad have some things to work out."

"We have to work out the fact that he was never a part of my life. He walked out on us when I was eight years old."

"I didn't know."

"No, you didn't. But I'm telling you this because I want you to know that I'm not my dad and I'm not going to walk out on my daughter."

At that moment he realized how much he wanted her to believe that about him. If she could believe in him, he might be able to believe a little stronger in himself.

"I know you won't."

He drew her hand to his lips and held it there. "Thank you."

Bailey walked into the living room the next day, the day after learning that Cody had his own past and lessons on letting go. Her dad was sitting in his recliner, his eyes closed and his breathing shallow and raspy.

His eyes flickered and he turned to smile at her, the gesture a weak attempt. Bailey wanted to hold on to him and keep him with her. She knew she couldn't.

"Dad, do you want to sit outside and watch Meg ride the buckskin?" She squatted next to his chair and covered his hand with hers.

In the last week she had watched him drifting away from her. She knew she couldn't bring him back. And she thought again about the conversation with Cody yesterday, when he had told her about his father, who hadn't really been a father.

Knowing this helped her to understand why Cody needed to do so much for Meg. She felt as if there were still missing pieces in the story of his life, things he had yet to share. Maybe he didn't want her to understand.

Her dad moved, bringing her back into his presence. He smiled at her, and for a moment she had hope. She sighed, knowing better than to let herself think he would get better.

"I'd like to sit outside." Her dad stood, wobbling as she slipped her arm around his waist, trying to pretend that it wasn't because he couldn't make it on his own.

They walked through the house, Jerry shuffling and Bailey keeping her steps small to match his. September had arrived and brought cooler weather. The fan on the porch made it almost too cool.

"Sit here, Dad, and I'll get you a pillow." She eased him into a chair.

"I don't need a pillow." His attention had already shifted to the corral and Meg. "I wanted it to be like this."

Bailey pulled the chain to turn off the fan and then sat down next to him. "Like what, Dad?"

"I wanted it to be a farm again, with horses and cattle and you not worrying about the future."

"It is a farm, Dad. We're going to make it."

She could have told him she still worried, just not over the finances. She worried about him not being there, and about Cody leaving and what that would do to Meg—and what it would do to herself.

At twenty-two she had felt something like love; maybe it had been a whisper or a promise of something that could have been special. Now, it felt different; it felt deeper, touching a different area of her heart. That frightened her because it also felt as if it could be gone tomorrow.

Laughter rippled across the lawn, Meg's childish tone and Cody's deeper one. Bailey watched as they rode double on the buckskin, not really liking that because the horse was young and sometimes flighty.

She had to trust Cody. He wouldn't do anything to hurt their daughter. That trust issue was becoming easier, but only because she was working on it.

"I sure love you, pumpkin." Jerry patted her arm.

"I love you, too, Daddy." She hadn't called him that in years. "Everything is going to be okay."

"I know it is." He smiled. "Don't be afraid to let Cody love you."

"Dad…"

"Honey, I know love when I see it, even if you don't."

She looked out at Cody and Meg, the little girl on the front and Cody behind her, his arms holding her secure. His arms made Bailey feel secure, too.

"I'm not afraid, Dad."

He nodded and closed his eyes. Bailey knew he needed to rest. He'd had a long night and he'd been in so much pain. She had wanted him to go to the hospital, but he'd argued that the hospital couldn't do anything.

Blue ambled up the steps and over to them. The dog nudged Jerry's leg and then his hand. Bailey turned her attention from her daughter to her father.

"Dad?" She touched his arm and then his neck as tingles of fear raced through her body. "Dad, wake up."

She heard Cody, knew he was running toward her. "Please, Dad, not yet."

It couldn't be time. She didn't want it to be now. She touched his neck, wanted there to be a pulse. When there wasn't, she started to tremble. She wanted to stop it all from happening. She prayed that God would change His mind.

Cody was there, holding her and Meg. Bailey couldn't move, not on her own, not away from her dad, because what if, what if he woke up, and what if this was all just a mistake?

"Bailey, we have to call the ambulance." Cody lifted Meg. "You have to come inside right now and take care of your daughter. She's the one who needs you."

Bailey nodded as she touched her dad's cheek. "Goodbye, Daddy."

She wasn't ready for him to be gone. She wasn't ready to be alone. But then, she wasn't. She felt Cody's hand on her back as he guided her into the house, Meg holding tightly to his neck. And she felt God's presence, touching her heart and letting her know that He would never leave her or forsake her.

Meg reached for Bailey, wrapping her arms around Bailey's neck as Cody went in search of the phone. The two of them sat at the dining room table, holding each other as Cody made the calls. Bailey wanted to feel, but everything drifted and she felt only numbness, removed from the action.

"Bailey, you've made arrangements, right?" Cody squatted in front of her, his eyes damp from tears. Real cowboys did cry. She had seen her dad cry more than once.

"I have. The coroner knows." She leaned and he moved toward her, drawing her against his chest as he stood.

"Take care of Meg, and I'll take care of the rest."

"I have to call people."

He put the phone in front of her and then walked outside, out to where her dad had finally found peace. From the window she could see the ambulance coming down the drive, Blue running next to it. There were no lights, no siren. There wouldn't be a need for those things.

She closed her eyes and said a silent prayer of thanks, that God had allowed her dad to leave this earth knowing that they would be okay.

Next she prayed she'd make it without him. The hole where

he used to be was already evident. Because he wasn't there to tell her everything would be okay.

To everything there is a season. A time for every purpose under heaven.

She closed her eyes and could almost hear her dad telling her that life had seasons. You don't plant tomatoes in the winter, he had once told her, and you don't prune in the summer. Every season has a purpose. God made it that way. Even the seasons of life.

"I don't want Grandpa to go." Meg whispered through her sobs.

"Neither do I, sweetie, but we have to let him go." Bailey hugged Meg to her as she dialed Lacey's number.

A time to be born, a time to die. A time to plant and a time to pluck what is planted. A time to kill. A time to heal. Her heart shook from within and tears burned her eyes again as she allowed the words she'd memorized as a kid to run through her mind.

A time to break down and a time to build up. A time to weep and a time to laugh. A time to mourn and a time to dance. A time to cast stones and a time to gather stones. A time to embrace and a time to refrain from embracing.

She couldn't go further, not with the ache growing inside her like a huge wound that would never be healed. A time to heal.

The hardest part, missing the person who was gone, missing what he'd been in their lives and the way he had kept hold of them, making everything right. And he'd held on until he knew that they would be taken care of.

The screen door creaked open. "Bailey, Pastor John is here."

Bailey nodded over her daughter's silky blond head. Her gaze connected with Cody's, and she remembered when he had been the empty hole in her heart. Now he was in her life, filling up the empty places.

A time to gain and a time to lose. She didn't know which was which, and her heart ached with gain and loss, and the knowing that loss would happen again.

It hadn't taken long for the community of Gibson to arrive, filling every empty space of the house and porch. Cody walked through the kitchen, crowded with church members and neighbors. The counters and table were laden with food, the aromas all blending together in a buffet of food smells. A lady with dyed black hair and ivory skin offered him something to eat.

"No, thank you. I'm going to check on Bailey."

The woman took hold of his arm and led him to a stack of plates. "Oh, sweetie, she's fine. She's with friends. Now, you take a plate and eat something. She'll need you soon enough."

He took the plate she placed in his hand, and he dutifully walked the line of food, knowing he wouldn't eat and being careful not to take much. As he walked out of the kitchen, he smiled in her direction, showing her that he'd done his duty.

Bailey was in the living room, surrounded by quiet conversation and the hum of air conditioners. She looked up as he walked through the door, and her mouth lifted in a slight smile. He tried to get to her, but a hand on his arm stopped him, a man he didn't know who wanted to talk about bull riding.

It was as if these people were protecting Bailey from him. He didn't like that. He didn't like the invisible circle around her or the way Meg leaned against her as if the world were ending. He wanted to take them both away from this and make them smile again.

He kind of figured Jerry would have wanted the same thing. He also knew it wasn't going to happen.

He left the house because there were things he could do outside and obviously nothing he could do inside. On his way out the back door he started to toss the plate in the trash, but through the window he saw Blue. She could do with a treat.

He walked past the groups that had gathered on the porch and the lawn. A few he spoke to as he passed, but he didn't stop. He went to the barn because Jerry was gone and the animals needed to be fed, and he didn't know what else to do.

He did know how to take care of animals. He started with the cats, mainly because they were all around his feet. The momma cat ran ahead of him. The kittens chased his boots, not caring that the shoes were attached to feet.

Blue was sitting next to the feed room, as if she approved of what he had decided to do. "It isn't like I can do anything else."

Blue wagged her tail and belly crawled in his direction.

Deep breath—shake it off. Cowboy up, Cody. He leaned against the rough wood post at the corner of a stall. Jerry wasn't gone. He just wasn't this side of heaven anymore.

What should he do? Cody knew the obvious answer. Feed the animals. And then what? Go inside with Meg and Bailey and pretend they really needed him. He knew the answer to that because he could hear the cars rolling down the drive as more neighbors and friends showed up to do the job of comforting.

His phone rang. He sighed as he flipped it open. This was going to be another person he didn't have answers for, another person he didn't want to let down.

"Mac." He scooped grain into a five-gallon bucket as they talked. "I know why you're calling and I plan on being back on tour in two weeks. We have a funeral this week, so that's the soonest I can get away."

He listened to one of his biggest corporate sponsors read him the riot act about money invested. Colson Farm Supply had been easier to deal with because they had supported his decision to get clean. Mac Farmer had investors who wanted a return on their investment. Cody didn't blame them.

"I'll be on tour, Mac, and I'll be at the finals."

Mac finished the conversation by telling him that they wouldn't be sponsoring him in the coming season. Cody slipped the cell phone back into his pocket and turned around.

Meg was standing in the door, tears streaming down her cheeks. He set the bucket of grain down and took her into his arms.

"Hey, kiddo, don't cry." That wasn't fair. He remembered all too well the number of times he had wanted to cry and his mom had told him that tears wouldn't fix anything. "You know what, you go ahead and cry and I'll sit here and hold you."

He sat down on the bench he had put in the corner of the tack room and Meg sat down next to him. She leaned against his side, hiccupping and wiping her eyes.

"I don't want you to leave." She hiccupped again. "I thought you were going to stay with us. I wanted us to be a family."

"We are a family, Meg. You have a mom and a dad who love you, and we're going to be here for you."

She shook her head and looked up at him with dark blue eyes overflowing with tears. "You said you were going to leave."

"I have to go do my job, but I'll be back."

"To live?" She was putting him on the spot, and he didn't know the right answer. He didn't want to lie to her.

"I can't live here with you, because I'm not married to your mom, but I'll come and see you a lot."

She slid out of his arms. "I don't want to miss you, too."

"I know, Meg." He didn't want to miss her, either. The thought of leaving kept getting harder.

She shot out of the barn with Blue on her heels. Cody watched to make sure she got to the house, and then he went back to where he'd left the bucket of grain. And he felt like a failure. He didn't know how to make it all better. He didn't know how to bring back Meg's smile. He didn't know how to convince her that he would always be there for her.

He'd just have to show her. Hadn't his grandfather always said something about the proof is in the pudding? He didn't know what it meant, not really, but he imagined it meant something about actions speaking louder than words.

He tossed scoops of grain into the feeders for the horses and went back into the barn for the fifty-pound bag he would give to the cattle. He heaved it over his shoulder and walked out to the trough. The cows were waiting, bawling at him as if they thought he should understand.

"You girls are mooing up the wrong tree. I don't know a thing about making women happy."

A fifty-pound bag of grain did the trick for the cows.

After he finished feeding, he closed the doors to the barn and walked back to his RV. He considered going to the house, but the yard was full of cars. Half the town of Gibson was crowded into the Cross home.

He was a part of Meg's life but not really in Bailey's life. Wasn't that what they wanted? What he wanted? He had done what he could for her. He had kept his promise to Jerry.

Now he was on his own again.

He walked into the kitchen of his RV and flipped on the light over the sink. He had a good view of the back porch, where people had gathered to talk and to share food. Bailey walked out the door and stood with a small group. He convinced himself she scanned the area, maybe looking for him.

Probably not. She had people around her who knew her and

whom she'd always known. He couldn't imagine a place for himself in that crowd.

He felt oddly outside the circle. But wasn't that what he wanted? Didn't he want to walk away without strings attaching him to her?

Meg—she was the thread that kept them connected, that would always connect them.

And he needed a drink. He needed an escape and a way to numb the pain. In the last eight months not once had it been such an overpowering need, sneaking up on him and taking hold.

He opened a cabinet door and rummaged through flashlights, cups and junk he should have thrown away a long time ago. Including the bottle at the back of the cabinet. He'd seen it a few weeks ago and had meant to pour it down the drain.

For some reason he hadn't.

He pulled it out, knocking over a flashlight and a few cups as he dragged it over the top of everything else. He hadn't emptied it because a part of him had probably wanted to keep it—just in case.

Perspiration beaded across his forehead, and he set the bottle down on the cabinet, setting a glass next to it. *Pour a drink, no one will know.* One drink wouldn't make him drunk or undo his sobriety. It would just be a drink to calm his nerves.

To numb the pain. He used to believe that. Now he realized it was a lie. The alcohol hadn't numbed his pain; it had made it worse. He hadn't dealt with problems back then; instead he had buried them.

He closed his eyes and when he opened them, he looked out the small window above the kitchen sink. Meg was on the swing, being pushed by a man Cody didn't know. The bottle gleamed amber and shimmering in the shaft of light peeking through the blinds that covered the window over the sofa.

Take a drink, give in. Or be strong. He remembered the lesson of Jesus fasting and the devil tempting Him to give up.

"God help me. I can't be strong on my own, but I have to be strong for Meg and Bailey." He took the lid off the bottle, lifted it and poured it down the sink.

"We are more than conquerors through Christ who strengthens us." He tossed the bottle in the trash and walked outside.

Meg looked up, her eyes rimmed with red from crying. She needed him sober. He needed that, too.

"Can I push my daughter?" He stepped behind the swing and the other man shrugged and walked away. Cody pulled the swing back and gave it a push. Meg laughed and asked him to push her higher.

"Anything for you, Meg."

Chapter Twelve

Three days later Bailey walked across the freshly mowed lawn of the cemetery. She could see the blue canvas shelter where others had already gathered, including an aunt and cousins she barely knew. At the church she had hugged them, shared words of sympathy, and somehow she had survived.

It didn't feel a lot like surviving.

Now, with Meg holding her hand and Cody walking on the other side, his hand close to hers, she tried to think about her dad, his life and what he would have thought of this solemn procession of people. He would have shook his head and told them to loosen up. He would have told them it was a beautiful fall day and they needed to watch the leaves change colors and hug their loved ones.

Jerry Cross would have loved the service at the church, when Gordy Johnson sang the good ole hymns and the congregation joined in. And after the message, Pastor John had allowed people to give short anecdotes about the Jerry Cross they'd known.

Meg had stood up and said that her grandpa always had

hugs. Bailey had cried and Cody had held her hand. She hadn't thought about it then, about Cody still being there when he didn't have to be. Now that she did stop and think, she was thankful for his presence. She was thankful for the day he stopped to apologize and then stayed because staying had been the right thing to do.

She looked at him now, in his black pants, gray shirt and tie. He looked strong. He looked uncomfortable in the tie. Her dad would have laughed at them all for dressing up.

What would he have said to her? She longed to hear his voice again, and his words of wisdom. But she could imagine what he'd say. Probably something about pulling herself up by her bootstraps and carrying on. He would have told her to remember all that God had done and to be strong in the Lord and in the strength of His might.

She had to stay strong for Meg. She had to be the person for her daughter that her dad had been for her. He'd left footprints in this life, footprints to live by.

Cody's hand settled on her back, and he guided her to the front of the tent. Try as she might, she couldn't remember all of her pep talks to herself about being strong, not at that moment with Meg holding her hand and the pastor saying final words of goodbye to a man who had been a part of their community and church for fifty-eight years.

It was hard to put it together, that the man they were talking about, the man who wouldn't be coming back to them was her dad.

A final amen brought it all to a close. Bailey accepted hugs and offers of help. Lacey held her tightly for a long minute and then let her go and walked off. The crowds thinned. Bailey's mind numbly registered the words, the hugs and Cody at her side.

What would her dad have said about Cody? For a moment she closed her eyes, allowing herself to trust the strength of the man next to her. That's what her dad would have told her. He would have told her to forgive and move on and that she didn't always have to be so strong.

She held tight to Meg as Cody guided them back to his truck. Tears started to fall, the tears she had kept in check for the last few hours. Now they fell—after she had convinced herself she was in control.

Cody lifted Meg into the truck before turning to Bailey. She wiped at her eyes with a tissue that was disintegrating. As she tried to turn away, Cody caught her and pulled her close. She didn't want to be held close, not when tears were pouring and she really needed a tissue.

"Let me see if I have a tissue or a towel in the truck." Cody touched her cheek and then he was in the truck, digging around and talking to Meg. He came back empty-handed.

"I'm fine." She wiped at her eyes with her hand and tried to cover her face.

"No, you aren't." He shoved his hands into his pockets again. "Nothing."

"It's okay. I'm fine."

"A man should have a handkerchief for moments like this." He jiggled his tie, the way he'd been doing all day, and then he smiled. With long fingers, he loosed the knot and jerked the tie over his head.

He held it out to her with a wink and a smile. "Will this do?"

She took the tie, their fingers touching and then they moved apart. She held the tie to her face, and then she glanced up at him again.

"You realize it'll be ruined?"

"I won't wear it again. Ties are for funerals and weddings."

She sniffled and raised the tie to her eyes. His words, considering everything else that was going on, shouldn't have upset her. Who cared if he never planned on wearing a tie again?

Maybe she wouldn't even miss him when he left? The thoughts were those of a woman at the end of her rope. The man standing in front of her must have guessed that she was at the meltdown stage. Before she could voice an objection, he pulled her close.

She wasn't alone. Cody's hands held her close and Meg was in the truck. They would get through this. They would move on with their lives. Cody whispered those promises into her ear, and she wanted to believe, almost believed because his faith sounded strong.

"I'm not going anywhere, Bailey. I'll be here as long as you need me."

She nodded against his chest, feeling the dampness of her tears on his linen shirt. As long as she needed him meant that a day was coming when he would be gone.

"Bailey, I mean that."

I love you, Bailey. Those had been his words next to a campfire in Wyoming. And she had believed him.

She nodded again because she knew he meant it, but she couldn't say the words that were trying to wiggle free. He would stay as long she needed, but she knew there were limits to his terms.

What if she needed him forever? It was really starting to feel as if she might.

A week went by before Cody felt it was the right time to discuss his schedule with Bailey. It had to be done. He had obligations to his sponsors and to the sport that had given him so much.

He had obligations in Gibson. For a man who had escaped ties, he suddenly had a truckload. He had a daughter. He had land. He had a career and people depending on him.

After a light rap on the back door, he walked into the kitchen. He no longer waited for an answer. Somehow this old farmhouse had started to feel like home.

And two months ago a thought like that would have made him itchy to be on the road. He would have doubted his ability to be the person they needed.

"Where's your mom?" Cody squatted next to the chair Meg sat in.

She was putting together a puzzle at the kitchen table. Instead of answering, she pointed down the hall. He stood and kissed the top of her head. Before he walked away, he squatted again.

"You okay, sweetie?"

She nodded again, but she didn't look up. His heart ached to make it all better for her, to make her smile again and to take away the hole in her heart, the place where she missed her grandfather.

He missed Jerry, too.

"My grandpa died when I was little." He pulled a chair close and sat down. The conversation had to go somewhere, but he was still grasping. "And after a while, I wasn't as sad anymore."

Meg nodded and she didn't cry. She was his in so many ways. "I'm glad he went to heaven, but I wanted him to stay with us and take care of us."

"He knew I would take care of you for him." He couldn't let Jerry down—that was a new fear. Could he ever be a man like Jerry?

"But what about when you leave?" She knew how to get to the heart of things. She got that from her mom.

"I promise I'll always come back."

She glanced away from the puzzle and cast what had to be a dubious expression at him. Another thing she'd learned from her mom. She was five and she already doubted him.

"Meg, I promise."

She nodded and went back to her puzzle. "I believe you."

"I have to talk to your mom now." He stood and for a long moment he stared down at his daughter. "I won't let you down, Meg."

She held his gaze, her eyes wide and maybe wise beyond her years. "Do you love us?"

Did he love them? He closed his eyes and nodded his head. He loved them with all his heart. He smiled at his daughter and she smiled back.

He walked out of the kitchen. Now to face Bailey. He almost thought she'd be easier than Meg.

"Bailey?"

"In here." Her voice sounded choked. That had happened a lot since Jerry's death.

But there were also good days, when she laughed and played with Meg. There were days she talked to him as if he was someone she wanted in her life.

He didn't know how to feel about that, or about how good or right it seemed to be that person. He could almost feel the roots digging in, wanting this to be the place where he landed for good.

Bailey was in her dad's room, sitting in front of the closet with boxes and bags. She looked up when he walked into the room. Today her eyes were dry. He didn't know how they could be, since seeing her surrounded by Jerry's belongings made him want to cry.

He sat down in the center of the piles of boxes and bags.

"I'm going through his things." She folded a shirt and stuck it in a garbage bag. "I keep talking to Meg about letting go and moving on. I think I need to lead by example."

He didn't want Meg to have to let go of anything. "I guess that's a good idea."

"It is." She folded another shirt, this time lifting it to her face for a moment before putting it in the bag with the other. "And what about you, Cody? You can leave, you know. We're fine now."

"I have land here, remember."

She nodded and continued to work through the pile of clothes. "I know and I've been thinking about that."

"Really?"

She moved to lean against the dresser, pushing aside a pile of things she'd been working on. "I thought that if I got things in order, I might be able to buy it back from you."

He rubbed the back of his neck as he tried to process that information. "Wow, I didn't expect that."

"Why? Look, we both know that this isn't what you want."

A year ago, six years ago, even two months ago, he might have agreed. Now he didn't know. Or maybe he did and he wasn't quite ready to process the information or what he was thinking and feeling. Good thing Bailey had it figured out.

"I guess neither of us knew me as well as we thought. I don't want to talk about this, because the conversation isn't going to go anywhere. The one thing I want to make perfectly clear, Bailey Cross, is that I'm in your life for a long, long time because I'm going to be a part of my daughter's life."

Tears pooled in her eyes and he regretted the sharpness of his words. When he tried to move close to her, she shook her head.

"No, I don't need that. You're right, and that was wrong of me."

"Not really. I've given you a lot of reason to doubt." He sat back again. "And the reason I came in to talk to you is because I have to leave. I have to make the next few events and the finals."

"I understand."

"Do you understand that I don't want to go?"

"Yes, I do, and I also understand why you're leaving. You've worked hard for this. You don't have to worry about us. We're used to taking care of things around here."

He worked this through his mind and wondered how much of it she meant and how much she was trying to convince him and herself that she didn't need him there.

"I might fly out Thursday to make the event in California. I might try to see my dad while I'm there."

Her face came up, her gaze meeting his. "You're going to see him?"

Of course it shocked her. It shocked him. How often did he mention his family? He spent more time trying to avoid that topic.

"Yes, I think it's time for us to work through some things."

She only nodded and he wondered if it would be selfish of him if he wanted her to be thinking about missing him. He shook free of that thought and the other that felt like missing her already. Lately he'd had a hard time remembering why he had been afraid of women who were looking for forever.

It seemed as if he might have been afraid of roots. Or afraid of being his father. In the last couple of months he'd proven to himself that he wasn't made in the image of Dalton Jacobs; he was made in the image of God, and the past no longer held him.

At least not in the way it once had. He was letting go. Bailey wasn't the only one learning that lesson.

"Wow, I didn't know he had these." Bailey held up pictures of her parents, obviously when they were newlyweds. Bailey looked like her mom.

It had been so many years since he'd seen his own mother, he couldn't remember what she looked like. He reached for a few of the pictures Bailey had already looked at. She watched him, but he could tell by the way she kept her face averted that she was pretending she wasn't.

"What about your family?" She finally asked. "I think there's more than you've told me."

What family? That wasn't really the answer she wanted. And he didn't want her sympathy. He had grown past that. Instead he moved from the floor to the edge of the bed, giving her back the pictures in his hands.

"My parents weren't—" He tried to think of the best way to explain. "They were divorced when I was little, and then they were busy living their own lives. No siblings and not a lot of extended family, especially once my grandparents were gone. We had a housekeeper named Maria."

Maria had cooked for him, taken care of him when he'd been sick and even gone to his school programs when his mother was out of town. When he turned eighteen and went to college, she went back to her family in California.

"I'm sorry." Bailey crossed her legs and leaned forward, nodding to let him know she wanted more.

"Bailey, it isn't a sad story of a little boy looking out the window, or whatever you're imagining. I stayed busy on the ranch and with the people who worked there."

"But it did affect you."

He could give her that. "Yes, it did. It made me worry that I couldn't be someone better than my dad."

"But you are."

"I hope." He softened his tone because he knew that Meg was a short distance down the hall. "And I hope you know that I won't let Meg down."

"I know that."

"And you." He didn't know why he said that or what he wanted from her.

"You don't have to worry about letting me down." She placed the pictures into the open cedar trunk.

"I promised your dad."

"That you would take care of us, and you have. You changed our lives and I'm so thankful for that. But now you're off the hook as far as your obligation to me."

"I'm off the hook? Bailey, I'm the father of your child. That's more than an obligation. That's something that ties us together."

"I don't want it to be a tie."

Shouldn't he feel relieved by that? He told himself that was the case, but he didn't feel it. He couldn't process what she was doing, but it felt as if she was handing him his freedom. As he got up to walk out of the room, he even told her a quiet "thank you."

Bailey waited until Cody was gone and she heard the front door click shut before she breathed a sigh of relief. In the last few days she had given this careful consideration, and she knew that the only way to deal with Cody was to let him go. She wouldn't let him lose the world championship over a promise he'd made to her dad.

Hearing her daughter ask if he loved them had really brought it all home. He hadn't answered. She had waited, breath held to hear what he had to say. And the answer had been left to her imagination. Did he love them? If he did, why hadn't he answered?

And why had she held her breath wanting to hear him say that he did?

Since he hadn't answered Meg, she had done what she thought best for them all. She had opened the door for him to leave. She knew that this new Cody took responsibility seriously, and she didn't want to be a responsibility in his life. Funny how in a matter of weeks, everything had changed.

At first she had worried that he would take Meg, and she had been jealous of his relationship with their daughter. She had worried that he would walk away and not come back. Now she didn't want to be the person he felt had held him back from what he wanted.

She didn't want to be the person he resented or felt obligated to.

At strange moments like this she remembered him hugging her close and telling her he'd stay as long as she needed him. And she had worried that her need for him might be "forever."

She needed to remember about letting go, and about a time to gain and a time to lose. Life had so many seasons and so many lessons to be learned. God was the ultimate teacher. She knew that in all of this He was teaching her to trust Him.

Ironically, she still seemed to be trying to control and make sure things worked out according to plan. As if God needed her help getting things done.

She stood and stretched. After two hours of working, she'd come a long way. She'd done a lot of letting go. Her dad's clothes were packed, old mementos were piled and photographs were tucked away in the cedar chest.

Cody was in the yard with Meg. Through the bedroom window she could see them at the swing. He didn't need to worry that he was the kind of dad who walked away.

As she walked out the back door, the rumble of thunder echoed overhead, clashing with the bark of the dog and the sound of a car engine on the highway. Bailey glanced toward the end of the drive and saw the car turning.

She recognized the long, blue sedan and knew that it belonged to an older couple from her church. She waited for them, wishing that they had called first. Exhausted emotionally, she really needed a break from condolences.

The car pulled to a stop. Bailey smiled and waved as the Bakers stepped out of the car to be greeted by Blue, who had managed to find a ball for them. They didn't smile back.

Dread tightened like a fist in Bailey's stomach.

Mr. Baker's stern gaze landed on Cody and Meg, and then it shifted back to Bailey with burning censure that placed an invisible scarlet letter on her chest.

"Ms. Cross, our pastor didn't feel a need to come and talk to you about your reputation, but we did."

Of course they did. Bailey didn't know if she should invite them into the house for tea or send them on their way. Cody had left Meg at the swing and was heading toward her with steady and meaningful steps.

This was a good time to show him she could take care of herself. She turned toward him, giving the Bakers her back for a moment while she grabbed hold of composure that was trying to flee under pressure.

"Cody, could you take Meg in for ice cream?"

He looked from her to the Bakers and back again to Mr. Baker. Cody didn't look like a man who wanted to back down. His mouth was set in a firm line, and his blue eyes flashed fire.

"Please." She made the word sound stronger than she felt. It would have been so easy to melt, and to let Cody take over.

"Fine, I'll be inside if you need me."

Bailey turned back to Mr. Baker, somehow gathering a smile and some courage for the coming lecture. If Pastor John didn't feel the need to bring it up, it had to be good.

"Ms. Cross, there are people in town who are concerned by this situation."

"Situation?"

"The fact that Mr. Jacobs is living here is the source of a lot of speculation and rumor. It isn't a fit environment for your daughter, nor are you setting a good example for her or other young people."

"Of course." Bailey wilted on the inside. "But you do understand that he's staying in an RV."

"We know that his RV is here."

But they didn't believe he slept in the RV. Bailey wanted to cry. She wanted to ask them if they understood what it meant to gossip, and how hurtful a sin it could be. She wanted to ask them if they had ever needed someone to stand in the gap and help them the way Cody had helped her.

She wanted to ask them if they had ever thought of being alone. Instead she smiled.

"I'm so thankful that you came here to warn me. Your concern is touching. It's hard to handle gossip but I'm sure the two of you will clear this up and let people know that Cody is living in the RV and he's only here temporarily."

Mrs. Baker came to life. "Of course we know that, dear. And we don't hold to gossip, and we hate to make someone else's business our own. We only came out of concern."

Bailey wanted to believe them. She wanted to not be hurt, but she couldn't shake off the pain. This moment meant another change in her life, and another letting go for herself and Meg.

The Bakers had just fast-tracked that moment she had been

dreading, the moment when Cody would leave. Because she knew that he wouldn't stay, not if he thought it would hurt Meg. And the gossip would hurt their daughter. If adults were talking, so were the children of those adults.

What if Meg went to school and one of the children in her class teased her? Bailey wanted to stop it all, to make it go away.

She wanted the Bakers to go away.

She smiled at them and thanked them for coming. They stood for a minute, staring at her as if they thought that continuing to stare might force her to come to her senses, or whatever they'd hoped to accomplish with their visit.

"I really do appreciate you coming out, and I will take what you've said into consideration."

"Goodbye then." Mr. Baker shook his head as he got into his car. His wife followed, her frown matching his.

Bailey breathed a sigh of relief as they started their car and backed out of the drive. And then she stood in the center of the yard not knowing what to do. She wanted to go to her dad for advice, but he wasn't there.

A soft whisper of a breeze, bringing the earthy scents of autumn swirled around her, reminding her of the source of strength she had that would never leave her. She closed her eyes, seeking peace.

"Did you straighten them out?" Cody touched her arm and she was tempted to lean back into his embrace. She wanted to let him handle it all and to know that he wouldn't leave.

She didn't want to be strong anymore. Not with Cody standing next to her.

Instead she turned to face him, finding it easier to smile than she would have imagined. His deep blue gaze traveled down the drive in the direction of the sedan just pulling onto the road.

"No, they set me straight about my tattered reputation and

the way I'm going to ruin my daughter's life by having you here with us."

"What do you think we should do? I know that moving the RV is on the top of the list." He looked away from her, his jaw clenching the way it did when he was working through a serious problem. When he turned back, she could tell he thought he had the answer. "Marry me, Bailey. Meg needs for us to be a family."

That was *so* not the answer.

Not fifteen minutes ago she had told him goodbye in a way that she thought released him from his mind-set of being responsible for them, that he had to keep a promise to her dad.

Now he was proposing.

Marry him, for Meg's sake, not because he loved her. It sounded good, like the right move. And it sounded like an alternative to the mess they'd made of things. But it didn't sound like the right answer.

It didn't sound like love or forever. And as much as she told herself it didn't matter, it did. In her heart, it mattered because right now she felt like that twenty-two-year-old young woman who had believed love could last forever and that Cody would be the one who made it happen.

"It would work, Bailey."

"No, I don't think so." Not without love, not if it was entered into as a solution to a problem or an answer to a promise he made to a dying man.

He brushed her hair back from her face and lifted her chin with his finger. The soft look in his eyes almost convinced her that maybe he wanted to marry her for the right reasons.

"It would solve everything." Wrong words if he meant to convince her.

"I'm not seventeen, Cody. I'm not a teenager who can't

take care of herself. Remember, you already solved that problem by buying the farm. Your job here is done."

"No, my job has just begun because my daughter is here. Don't forget that important factor in this equation."

"I've been very aware of her for nearly six years."

"While I wasn't here." He brushed a kiss across her cheek and stepped away. "I guess if I was you, I'd have doubts, too."

Bailey nodded but she didn't answer. She didn't have to think about his proposal. She didn't want him to marry her just to solve a problem. The horses whinnied to her, a call for their evening meal. Bailey walked to the barn because that was easier than dealing with the mess she'd made of things. As she worked, she glanced in the direction of the RV.

Cody was loading the lawn furniture into the back of his truck and rolling in the awning of the RV. Meg followed behind him, seeming to fear he might never come back. At least Blue stayed next to Bailey. She still had the dog.

The cows had come up. Bailey walked out the back door of the barn into the bright sunlight, squinting as her eyes adjusted. Blue circled the cows, barking as Bailey pulled the string to open one end of the feed bag and emptied it into the trough.

She could hear banging as Cody readied the RV to leave. She didn't want to picture the look on her daughter's face. She remembered all too well what it had felt like to watch Cody Jacobs drive away.

After the RV was loaded and hooked to the truck, Cody came to say goodbye. He had changed into a clean polo shirt and had replaced his cowboy hat with a ball cap. He hadn't shaved.

"I'll be back in a week or so. Pastor John is going to let me park the RV at his place for the night."

"We'll be here." Bailey had hold of Meg's hand, but Meg pulled free and rushed into Cody's arms.

"I don't want you to go." She cried into his sleeve while he held her close.

"I know, sweetie, and I don't want to go. But remember, this is my job. Sometimes I have to go, but I'll always come back."

"Promise?"

"I promise." He kissed the top of her head and stood. His dark blue eyes sought Bailey's and he stepped close.

Bailey waited, not sure how their own goodbyes would go. They didn't hug, or even touch. He smiled and told her they'd probably talk before he left for California; and then he walked away, teaching her another lesson about letting go, this one feeling a lot like the one in Wyoming years ago.

Chapter Thirteen

"What's wrong with you today?"

Bailey turned at Lacey's question. They'd just worked through a seriously busy lunch shift, so there hadn't been a lot of time for talking. There definitely hadn't been a moment for Bailey to tell her friend about the previous day.

The proposal and the goodbye were still fresh on her mind. She didn't know how to mention it or what to say. Now Lacey was standing in front of her in the waitress station, effectively blocking any escape Bailey might have planned.

"What do you mean, what's wrong with me?"

Bailey could think of a list of things that were going wrong in her life, but she could think of more things right. At this moment she really needed to count her blessings.

"What's wrong with you? It's a simple question. I know you've had a rough few weeks, but this morning you came in with a snarl, and your eyes were puffy."

"Allergies."

"Yes, of course, allergies." Lacey fiddled with her apron, and when she looked up, there wasn't a smile. "How's Meg doing in school?"

"She's doing great. It took me a few days to adjust."

"How's Cody?"

Bailey poured herself a cup of coffee and stirred in a spoon of sugar, taking her time because she needed time. How was Cody? Gone? Out of her life? That was all way too melodramatic. Lacey moved from her post at the door and leaned on the counter next to Bailey.

"He's leaving." Bailey lifted her coffee and took a sip. "But from the look on your face, maybe you know more than I do."

"I do know about the trip the Bakers made to your house yesterday."

"That was a lovely time. Why didn't you just say that you knew?"

"I didn't want to force you to talk."

Bailey laughed at that, a real laugh that felt good. "Oh, so now you're tactful."

"I'm always tactful, and considerate." She smiled a sweet, too-sweet, smile. "And I guess that's why Cody's RV is at the pastor's house."

"Yes, it is." Bailey just wanted to sit with a cup of coffee. Preferably by herself. The bells on the door clanked, giving her a much-needed escape. "Oh, that's my customer."

"Chicken."

"You betcha."

Bailey shot a smile over her shoulder as she hurried to seat the customers and offer them menus. When she walked back to the waitress station, Lacey was filling ketchup bottles so the evening waitresses would have a stocked supply.

"Finish the story." Lacey didn't give her a break. "What happened?"

"He proposed." Bailey sort of enjoyed dropping that on her

friend. She walked off with a carafe of coffee and two glasses of iced water.

"Hey, come back here."

Bailey shook her head as she walked across the diner to the corner booth that her customers had picked. She filled their coffee cups and set the water glasses in front of them as they scanned the menu.

They spent five minutes looking at the menu and then ordered the special. Bailey hurried back to the kitchen with the order, but then she took her time returning to where Lacey was waiting for her. She wasn't quite ready to talk about her very first proposal and why it had hurt so much to hear the words *marry me.*

"He proposed." Lacey didn't wait for her to walk to the waitress station.

Bailey cringed, wondering how many people had heard. She lifted a finger to her mouth to quiet her friend.

"A sympathy proposal, that's all."

"Sympathy. What does that mean? A gorgeous man proposed and you turned him down because you thought he felt sorry for you?"

"I turned him down because he offered it as a way to solve our problems. Marriage would give Meg a family unit and stop the gossip. End of story."

"You said no? Forgive me if I don't understand turning down a man you're in love with and a man that is the father of your daughter."

"I can't base a marriage on what happened in Wyoming. I can't marry him because it would be the easy thing to do."

"But you love him."

The bells on the door were clanging again. Bailey and Lacey looked at one another; neither made a move toward the dining area.

"I won't be the person he resents, Lacey. I won't tie him to me that way."

"Why would he ever resent you?"

"Because he made a promise to my dad to take care of us. I don't want him to think that marriage is what my dad expected. Cody did what he had to. He bought the land. He's been here for us. He doesn't need to watch over me the rest of my life. I think it is time for us both to move on."

"Maybe he really wants a life with you?"

"That isn't what he wanted before, and I don't think it's what he wants now."

"How do you know that, Bay?"

Bailey opened the cooler door and pulled out two salads and a caddy with salad dressings. Lacey was ready with a tray, and a sympathetic smile.

Bailey shrugged. "Maybe I don't want to regret him again."

She regretted him.

Cody had stopped by the Hash-It-Out to say goodbye. He had gotten more than he'd bargained for. He'd gotten to hear what Bailey thought about him and their relationship. He was the person she regretted.

Of course he was. How could he not be on the list when he had been the person who had walked out on her and had left her to raise a daughter alone?

A daughter he hadn't known about, he reminded himself.

But that didn't undo what he'd heard her say. She didn't want to regret him. She meant the proposal and marriage. That had been a mistake, to propose spur of the moment as a way out for them both.

He should have known better. He should have told her that in the last few weeks, he'd been thinking of forever with her.

People were staring because he was standing in the dining room of the Hash-It-Out, holding his hat in his hands. He looked around the sparsely populated room, smiled at the few customers and shoved his hat back on his head.

He didn't want to be a regret in someone's life. He had enough regrets of his own.

He walked out of the diner and got back into his truck. For now he would drive over to the house and say goodbye to Meg. School had gotten out early and one of the ladies from church had picked her up and taken her home.

Telling Meg goodbye would be one of the hardest goodbyes of his life. Bailey probably wouldn't believe him, but saying goodbye to her in Wyoming had topped the list. Back then he hadn't wanted to get tangled up in something from which he couldn't escape.

Now he was tangled in more ways than one. And nothing had changed. He hit the steering wheel, looking for an out for his frustration and it didn't work. She didn't own the copyright on regret.

He wouldn't go where his mind wanted to go, to old habits and a way to numb himself against the emotions he didn't want to handle. His mind did go there, though, for a brief moment, trying to convince himself that he could deal with this if he drowned himself in alcohol.

Shaking off those thoughts, and the sharp edge of temptation, he gripped the steering wheel tightly and made a deep reach for strength.

The road to Bailey's took him past the land he'd bought. Land with green grass, gently rolling hills and a year-round spring. Bailey's land. Probably a good reason for resenting him. He had her land, the land she hadn't been able to save from foreclosure.

Cody took a deep breath and let it out. He wouldn't go backward, doubting himself and giving in to temptation. He felt it on the inside, a strength that didn't come from himself.

He hadn't let down Bailey or Meg.

And he wouldn't. He wouldn't marry Bailey. She was right: The proposal had been for the wrong reasons. He hadn't thought it through. He'd just been trying to do the right thing.

He'd been wrong on so many levels.

Pulling into the drive of the farm and seeing Meg on her swing, he knew one thing he wasn't wrong about. He wasn't wrong about wanting to be a part of his daughter's life. A big part.

She saw him coming and jumped off the swing mid-arc, landing on her bottom but laughing as she jumped and ran toward his truck. He slowed to a stop and opened the door.

"Hey, kiddo."

He climbed down and lifted her into the air. Blue barked and out of the corner of his eye he saw Elsbeth Jenkins watching from the porch. He waved.

"I miss you," Meg said as she leaned her head against his shoulder; he wondered how this had happened. Two months ago he had been on his way to the next event, and now he had this little girl and she missed him.

He didn't know if anyone before had ever missed him when he left. A few had been angry with him. He closed his eyes and held Meg close. And some had regretted him. Being missed and loved like this was a whole new feeling.

"I missed you, too."

"I don't want you to go away."

He put her down and took hold of her hand to lead her over to the swing. They walked side by side, and when he looked down, she was watching and trying to match her steps with his.

They sat down on the bench swing, and she leaned into his side, five years old and totally trusting. He hoped she would never lose that trust and that no man would ever come along to make her regret.

"Meg, I have to go, but I'll be back. Soon."

"Before school is out?"

"Before Thanksgiving."

"Is that when school is out?" She looked up, her eyes blue and large.

"It's less than six weeks." He lifted her hand and looked at her small fingers. "And I'll be here for Christmas."

She didn't respond. Her gaze shifted to the barn, like she was trying to think of something. Blue had joined them and the dog's head rested on Meg's knees.

"Do you think my mom will be done being mad at you by then."

"I sure hope so."

Speaking of Meg's mom, there was Bailey, driving down the road in the new truck she'd bought the previous week. Cody stood and Meg joined him. He smiled down at her and then they walked across the yard together. This time he matched his steps to hers. She looked up and smiled before taking a giant step, which he pretended he couldn't match.

"I didn't expect to see you here." Bailey spoke to him but she leaned down to kiss Meg on the cheek. "Hey, sweetie, did you have a good day?"

Meg's eyes watered and she looked from Cody to Bailey and then back again, as if she expected him to do something. The problem with that was that he'd already tried something, and it hadn't worked.

Now he had to find a way to show her that he wanted her in his life for reasons that made sense—not to just fix a problem.

"I came to say goodbye."

Bailey stood up, nodding at his announcement. She probably didn't think he would come back.

"We'll be watching. And praying."

That he wouldn't be hurt. "I appreciate that."

He took in a deep breath and told himself this was for the best. Goodbyes didn't used to be so hard.

"Be careful." Bailey had hold of Meg's hand. "Meg, tell your dad goodbye."

Meg rushed into his arms and he held her tightly.

"This isn't goodbye, Meg. This is, *I'll see you soon.*"

He ignored Bailey because he knew that look in her eyes. He wanted to believe she was sorry he was leaving. Instead he told himself she was glad to see him go.

Bailey walked through the doors of the tiny Gibson post office. The building smelled like old paint and pine cleaner. It hadn't changed in years. And from behind the counter, Mary Walker was still watching the town like a hawk.

An easy, in-and-out operation wasn't going to happen; Bailey knew that the minute Mary spotted her. Bailey tried the avoidance maneuver: Keep eyes averted; pretend you haven't been seen. She put fifty cents into the stamp machine and pushed the button. Nothing came out.

A quick flick of her gaze in the direction of the counter and she could see Mary leaning, trying to get a good look at her. Bailey pulled her shirt down, flattening it. She was not pregnant.

That was the new rumor.

The door opened. Bailey kept her attention focused on the nonworking stamp machine. That thing had been in the Gibson post office since before her birth. No wonder it didn't work.

"Give it up, Bay. You're going to have to buy a stamp from Mary." Lacey nudged Bailey's shoulder and laughed.

"I'll cook you dinner if you'll buy it for me."

"No way—and ruin all of Mary's fun?" Lacey glanced in Mary's direction and waved. "It'll all blow over."

"I've been saying that for two weeks." The rumors had started after Cody left.

"Yes, I know, and it really is starting to die down. You know that people love you and care about you. A few people needed something to talk about, and those few are getting straightened out by the rest of us."

"And I appreciate that."

"I'll buy your stamp. But I want shrimp on the grill and we'll watch bull riding together."

Bailey grabbed Lacey's arm. "I'll cook the shrimp and we'll watch a movie."

Lacey blocked Mary's view. "Why can't we watch bull riding?"

"Because I don't want to watch him get hurt." There, she'd said it, and nothing bad had happened. She had admitted that she cared.

Lacey should have been happy. She'd gotten her way. Instead there were tears in her eyes and a look of sympathy on her face.

"Bailey, I'm so sorry that I teased you." She wiped at her eyes. "I'm a horrible friend."

"You're a good friend. But I can't watch. I can't let Meg watch."

Hopefully Lacey would leave it at that and not ask her to explain why it mattered. Those were questions Bailey didn't want to answer, not even to herself.

She knew what she had to do. She had to move on. She wouldn't let herself spend a year moping. She was older and wiser; she was good at letting go.

"Then we'll have shrimp and play on the swing." Lacey glanced in Mary's direction. "Let me get you a stamp and I'll be right back. I'll even buy the shrimp."

As much as it hurt to let go, Bailey realized how good it felt to have friends who cared. It felt good to know that she was strong enough to move on. Again.

She smiled at what had to be a reflection of her new strong self. "Shrimp and a stamp and no lectures?"

"Only twenty questions." Lacey smiled as she walked away.

"Fine, but I'm not answering." Bailey bit down on her lip and blinked away the tears that surfaced. She was strong enough to move on.

Chapter Fourteen

❦

"What a bull." Cody whistled as he saw the animal run into the chute. The chute that meant the animal was meant for him to ride.

Jason laughed. He could laugh. He wasn't the one who would be riding that wild beast in five minutes. This one could make him or break him, literally. He didn't like the broken part. Not now, when he was riding healthy and heading for the finals next week.

It was the end of October. Missing Meg and Bailey had created a deep ache in his heart. He hadn't expected that. He hadn't expected his thoughts to drift to Gibson on a regular basis.

"Buddy, you'd better get your mind off Missouri and on that killer bull you've got in the short go."

The short go was the round that the highest scores for the event took part in. It determined the champion of the event and who took home the big check. He was in fourth overall and he could easily win. Riding this bull, not so easy.

"My mind *is* on riding." Cody slipped a glove on his riding hand.

"You left your heart in Gibson, Missouri."

"Stop with that."

Cody pushed past his friend, wanting to say a whole lot more than "stop." He'd taken so much from his friends; he had lost his reputation for being cool and untouchable.

The announcers were calling him Moony because they said he was mooning over a woman he'd left behind. They didn't know the half of it.

The farther he'd driven from Missouri, the more he'd realized his mistake. Mistakes, plural. He'd made more than one. And soon enough he'd have to go back and face them. He couldn't get out of it. He was going to be her neighbor.

"I'm going to ride this bull, and then I'm going to deal with you." He hoped Jason knew he meant it. Jason only laughed.

"I like this new side of your personality that isn't fuzzy with alcohol. You're a lot easier to goad. A lot edgier."

Cody managed a smile. He liked sober, too. He liked vibrant colors and being in control of his emotions. Even if the emotions were twisting inside him.

"Yeah, I'm glad I could make things more fun for you."

Jason grabbed Cody's bull rope, which wasn't cool, because it was time for him to head for the chute, and the bull that waited for him.

"Tell me something, Cody. Are you in love?"

"I love my daughter." His heart ached, remembering that last hug. And remembering the look in Bailey's eyes. "I'm the man that Bailey Cross regrets."

"Oh, come on, are you still holding on to that? Don't you know that women say one thing and mean something totally different?"

"I've heard that." He jerked the bull rope out of Jason's hand. "I have a bull to ride."

"You have a woman you need to make amends with."

"You're a good one to talk. Don't you have a woman in Oklahoma that you haven't talked to in a year?"

"Yeah, but that's different; she knows I love her."

Cody shot Jason a look and his friend only laughed. Cody didn't have time for laughing. He had to get on a big black bull that had a reputation for being mean.

The bull snorted, bucked and moved into the side of the chute as Cody slid onto his back. Jason helped by pulling the bull rope tight. That was the great part about the sport, the way competitors helped one another and prayed for one another. What other sport had men in direct competition cheering one another on?

Cody wrapped the bull rope around his hand. The bull, ready for the fight, jumped and tried to go out the end of the chute. Jason caught Cody by the back of his Kevlar vest and kept him from going headfirst into the bars of the chute.

"If I don't make it off this thing alive, make sure Bailey gets the deed to that land." He was half-joking as he made the comment to Jason. Jason didn't smile.

Cody nodded and the gate opened. The bull came out of the gate spinning, twisting and doing a belly roll that felt as if it was jerking Cody's spine out of his back. He tilted his head down and prayed he'd make it to the buzzer, and then out from under the bull's hooves.

The roar of the crowd combined with his heaving breath, and the bull's snorting breath. Slobber and dust swirled, the grime settling in his eyes.

The buzzer sounded and it was all over. Faintly, he heard people screaming. He caught a glimpse of Jason on the chute, waving and shouting, laughing as he cheered Cody on.

The ground swept around him in a blur, and there didn't

seem to be a soft spot to land. One of the bullfighters ran in front of the bull and yelled that he had it covered. That meant he'd distract the bull while Cody jumped. That's what bullfighters did; they took the hit so the rider could make a safe getaway.

Cody jumped, landing clear. Sigh of relief, and then a yank on his arm that delivered him from relief in less than one second. His hand was hung up and the bull was still running. He hated that he'd been here before—back in January, in the wreck that changed everything. He didn't want a flash of memory that felt a lot like panic as he tried to stay on his feet.

The bullfighters were there, telling him to stay on his feet. Like he didn't know that he needed to stay on his feet. He hopped and ran alongside the spinning, running fifteen-hundred-pound bull. The bullfighter clung to the other side of the bull, trying to loosen the rope, which was wrapped like a viper around his hand. He caught a glimpse of Jason and a few of the others, hats in hands, praying.

The bull turned, spinning back on him and kicking in the process. Cody's hand slid free as the bull gave him a hefty push with his mammoth head and rammed him into the ground.

And the only thing he could think about was why he loved Bailey and how he wanted to make things right. If only he knew what that meant.

Bailey had cleaned out almost the entire house, throwing away things they'd kept for years for no reason and boxing up other items she couldn't part with. Which was what had created the surplus of junk in the first place. Who kept stuff like this, ancient postcards from places they couldn't remember, and cards from birthdays twenty years in the past?

From the kitchen she could hear Meg and Lacey laughing

at something they'd concocted, probably another batch of homemade dough to make silly creatures. The kitchen table was full of baked dogs, cats and horses. They'd have to clear it off soon, so they would have a place to eat lunch.

The homemade dough had been a way to distract Meg since last Friday night's bull ride, when Meg had watched the ride on TV and saw her father get injured.

Bailey still felt a thread of guilt because she and Lacey had been preoccupied with an out-of-control flame in the grill and hadn't realized that Meg had turned on bull riding. Or that she'd watched her daddy get hurt.

Cody had been unconscious when they carried him out of the arena on a stretcher. Meg had run from the house, crying because her daddy wasn't moving. Bailey and Lacey had hurried into the house in time for a replay of the ride. And a third replay, and then a fourth. Each time they showed it, her heart clenched with fear. Watching it, Bailey had realized just how much she didn't want to see Cody hurt.

Together they had prayed, and Meg had refused to leave Bailey's side for the rest of the night.

Fortunately a concussion had been his only injury. It had been serious but not life threatening. And he had called them from the hospital because he hadn't wanted Meg to be upset.

Bailey pushed away other feelings because she didn't want to deal with all of this, not right now. She was packing up junk from the past. The past with Cody didn't need to be unboxed for a second look.

Wyoming, like old postcards and letters, needed to be boxed up and put away. For good. She hated that she'd found a box of pictures from that summer.

With Meg safe in the kitchen with Lacey, Bailey sifted through the pictures. She tried to remember the names of people she'd forgotten. She stopped to linger on a picture of herself with Cody.

Even now it looked like love. She reminded herself of his goodbye, then, when he'd told her that cowgirls always think they're in love. And this time when he'd said goodbye with a makeshift proposal.

"Hey, the mailman just stopped. Want me to go out and get it?" Lacey yelled from the kitchen.

"Sure."

Bailey knew that meant Meg joining her in a minute. She didn't want to explain the pictures and what looked like a happy young couple. She tossed them in the box and pulled the lid closed just as Meg jumped through the door yelling "Boo."

Bailey put a hand to her heart and pretended to scream. Meg laughed, and it was good for Bailey to see her laugh again. The hole in their lives was getting smaller. They still missed Jerry. They still felt the emptiness of the place he used to inhabit, but each day it got easier to go on.

And missing Cody was a thing of the past. Regret was in the past. Bailey hugged Meg and held her close. The screen door slammed shut and Lacey's sandaled feet clicked on the tile as she headed their way.

"Letter for you." Lacey tossed the real mail to Bailey. Lacey took the junk mail and Meg. "Looks like you might need a minute to look that over."

Bailey glanced down at the business envelope with the return address of a lawyer in Oklahoma. Her heart ka-thumped against her chest, and fear sent fingers of dread up her spine.

What had Cody done? She closed her eyes and said a prayer because she didn't want this to be about her original fears, that he'd take her daughter away. She slid her finger under the flap and pulled the letter out.

As she read, her eyes watered and her heart raced to keep up with her emotions. She read the papers again and then closed her eyes, trying to make sense of it all.

"What's up?" Lacey said from the doorway.

"Where's Meg?"

"Watching a movie. I told her to stay and I'd make cookies. The kind we can actually eat."

"Thank you." Bailey wiped her eyes.

"Gonna share?" Lacey sat on the floor next to her.

"It's a letter from Cody and from his lawyer. He doesn't want to be someone I'll regret." She blinked away tears but couldn't blink away her own regret. It stuck in her heart, forcing her to deal with what she'd been running from.

Her past. The part that couldn't be put in a box.

"Well?" Lacey reached for the letter and Bailey handed it over.

"He's signing the land back over to me, putting it in my name and Meg's."

"What's this about regret?" Lacey read over the letter, glancing up when she read the last line.

"I don't know."

"Do you regret loving him?"

Bailey shrugged, but she knew the answer. She resented being hurt. She regretted things they'd done, and said. She didn't regret having him in her life—except when it hurt and except when she had to get over him.

She didn't want him to walk away, and she didn't want him to be just the guy who picked up her daughter for weekends. Unfortunately that was the person he was in her life, and she needed to deal with it.

"I can't let him give that land back to me. It's his and he deserves it."

"And you want him close at hand. Why, Bailey? So he can be here for you in a way that is safe and comfortable?"

Bailey was reaching for the phone but Lacey's comment stopped her. "What does that mean?"

"It means you like safe. You like comfortable. You like to be in control. Cody undoes all of those things in you. He takes over. He makes you feel uncomfortable because you know you love him and you don't want to give in to that emotion. He definitely isn't safe."

"Thank you for that, Dr. Phil."

"Glad I could help. So this means you like a safe place to land, and your daughter needs a safe place to land. And Cody is it, but you don't want him to be."

"He proposed because he wanted to protect us, not because he loves me." She glanced over the letter again. "I don't want to be the person who trapped Cody Jacobs. I want to be the woman someone wants to love forever."

"Whatever."

"Whatever, what?"

"A man doesn't hand over a quarter of a million dollars if he doesn't love a woman."

"He loves his daughter and I'm giving the land back." She had the phone and she dug through a pile of magazines for the phone book, which she'd accidentally tossed into the throwaway pile.

"What are you doing now?"

"Calling the airport."

"Because?"

Bailey shot Lacey a look that did nothing but make her smile. "I'm going to Vegas to give this back to him and to tell him I don't regret him."

Lacey stood up. "I'm going to go play with Meg. At least she's honest about loving Cody."

Chapter Fifteen

Cody flipped his phone closed because it was obvious Bailey wasn't answering. He'd been trying all day. Time to put it away and let it go.

"What's up? Still can't get hold of her?" Jason had walked up behind him.

They were scheduled to sign autographs in the hotel lobby. He had thirty minutes to shower and get changed. Jason had fallen onto the bed and was kicked back like he planned to take a nap. Cody slapped his friend's boots off the bed.

"Get a room."

"I'm your roommate, remember? You have money and I'm this year's biggest loser."

"You don't try hard enough. You're not hungry."

"Okay, so my weekly allowance makes me weak. Think I should give it up?"

Cody laughed. "Nope, I think you should get a sweet wife and buy a farm of your own."

"Nope, not this cowboy. I'm going to leave settling down to guys like you. The more of you that I can get married off, the better my chances are going to be. Last week's knock on the head proves that romance takes the edge off the cowboy."

Cody rubbed his head. The bruise was still there, a dark spot on his forehead, right at his hairline. It could have been worse.

The bump on his head was the least of his concerns. Where was Bailey, and why did he feel panicked at the thought of not being able to reach her? He flipped his phone open again and dialed, again.

One ring, two; it was answered on the third. He sighed with relief until he realized it wasn't Bailey on the other end.

"Lacey?"

"You got it, cowboy."

He paused and she laughed, answering his unspoken question. "Caller ID—remember we live in the modern age of technology. Says right here, Love of Her Life. Oh, wait, no, it says Cody Jacobs. Sorry, she isn't here."

The woman talked nonstop. Cody smiled, for a second missing her. He missed Gibson. He closed his eyes, the biggest longing still hitting home, right in the region of his heart.

He missed Bailey. He missed her smile and the way she made him think about forever. He missed her in his arms.

"Where is she?" He turned his back on Jason's knowing grin. Jason should meet Lacey; that'd put a stop to his roaming. It would put a stop to his endless teasing of Dr. G.

"She's on a trip. She decided she and Meg needed a little time away from the farm."

"What about school?"

"Kindergarten, cowboy. They're not real strict with absenteeism at that age, and they let her take her work with her."

"Where are they?"

Long pause. He waited. "Lacey, are you still there?"

"Still here, but I'm creating a long pause, hoping you'll get off my case. She isn't here. She's on a trip. Let me see, yes, that's all she told me."

Cody flipped the phone shut and slid it into the front pocket of his jeans. Jason sat up and flipped off the television.

"Time to go, loverboy."

Cody picked up a magazine and gave it a good toss at his friend. "I hope you fall in love someday so I can give you a hard time."

The words slipped out and Cody couldn't move. Jason looked just as surprised, with his mouth hanging open and his eyes wide. Cody figured he probably looked just as shocked as Jason. He hadn't planned those words, and he hadn't thought about saying them until that moment.

No, that was a lie. He was lying to himself. He hadn't called it love, but he had thought about what he had been feeling and the way he missed Bailey. He had told himself he was just missing Meg, and Gibson.

He felt roots digging down deep, the kind that didn't choke the life out of a person. He'd been pruned for a reason, to make the roots stronger.

"Wow, you didn't expect that, did you?" Jason threw a pillow and hit Cody in the face. He didn't even try to block it.

He sank onto the edge of the bed, gut-stomped worse than any bull had ever done. He loved Bailey Cross. And he had proposed to make things easier for her. What a lie that had been. He wanted to marry her because he loved her.

"I can't think about this right now. This is the last night of the finals. If I let myself get caught up in this, I won't be able to think."

"By *this* you mean love, right? Or are you too much of a man to say the word?"

Cody stood and reached for his hat, his favorite black hat.

He pulled his jeans down over the tops of his boots and rolled the sleeves of his shirts down to button at his wrists.

"We need to go."

"So this is what love looks like."

Cody walked out the door, ignoring the guy who used to be his best friend laughing behind his back. Cody smiled as he pushed the down button on the elevator.

When he walked onto the floor of the lobby, there was a huge crowd already gathering. Tables had been set up to sell posters, hats and other souvenirs. People milled, waiting for autographs. There were women in high heels and high hair, wearing vests and cowboy hats. Kids wore leather vests and boots. Kids wore chaps and carried yellow-and-red lariats.

It was the same as every other year he'd been there. The air was charged with excitement, most of it coming from the riders who were ready to ride, not ready to sit and think or talk about riding.

The atmosphere was the same as every other year, and not. He was the man that Bailey Cross regretted, and she was the best thing that had ever happened to him.

Only he hadn't realized it until it was too late.

Meg had hold of a balloon and a poster of her very own daddy. And she wanted everyone to know it. There was only one problem: That meant that everyone was staring at Bailey, smiling and wondering who in the world she was and why she was here.

Here, as in Vegas. She was wondering the same thing. What in the world had she been thinking when she made that plane reservation and hopped on a flight across the country, far from home and safety?

Being this close to Cody, even if she hadn't seen him, didn't feel safe. It felt disconcerting because that's what she always felt around Cody.

"Mom, do you think he isn't here? What if he went home?"

By *home* Meg meant Gibson. Bailey didn't want to tell her daughter that Cody wasn't in Gibson. She didn't want to hurt Meg with the truth, that Cody was doing his best to detach from them. Why else would he send her a deed to that land?

He was tired of playing house. He was breaking the connection with them. If she had the land back, he wouldn't have to stay in Gibson, keeping a promise he'd made to her dad.

Bailey's heart broke for Meg. She told herself that it was for Meg that she'd cried and for Meg that she felt that emptiness all over again. It was as if she was holding her newborn daughter, wondering if she would always be raising her alone.

Why had she allowed her guard to drop and her heart to believe that Cody would be a real part of their lives? Meg's hand tightened on hers. A real part of Meg's life, she reminded herself. This wasn't about Bailey and Cody; it was about Cody and Meg.

"There's a man with a camera."

Meg pointed at the man heading in their direction. He wore a polo with the logo of a major sports publication and a gleam in his eye that said he thought he had a story.

Bailey turned, knowing now that Meg's announcement earlier that Cody was her daddy had been heard by the wrong people. That made everything more complicated. Bailey only wanted to give Cody back the deed or the intent letter that said he was signing the land over. Whatever it was, she wanted him to have it back. For Meg.

She wasn't about to let Cody Jacobs walk out of their lives, not without a fight. Not this time.

Now there were people staring and whispering. That seemed

to be her lot in life. Someone touched her arm. Bailey jerked away, not wanting to be caught here like this.

"Bailey, come with me." Willow was at her side, a friendly smile in a crazy world far from Gibson, with its quiet streets and gentle pace.

"Where's Cody?" Bailey had hold of Meg's hand and Willow had hold of Bailey's arm. They were rushing through the crowd, away from the camera.

"We'll find him, but for now we have to get the two of you out of the spotlight." Willow's pace slowed. "Unless you're okay with being interviewed."

"I'm not at all okay with that." She smiled down at her daughter. "Meg was excited. She didn't realize Cody had posters."

Willow laughed, the sound soft and friendly. "I heard. Everyone heard. She's proud of her daddy. Nothing wrong with that. The only problem is that Cody is a legend when it comes to relationships and his personality. You know what I mean."

"Yes, not everyone knows that he's changed. And no one knew about Meg until today."

"That's big news."

"Mom, where's my dad?" Meg's little legs were hurrying to keep up.

"Not here yet, sweetie."

Willow rushed them into an elevator. "You can hide out in my room until the dust settles. And later, I'll make sure you have good seats at the arena."

"Thank you." Bailey kept hold of Meg as they stepped onto the floor that housed the penthouse suites. Willow didn't travel inexpensively.

Willow inserted a card in the door and it clicked open. She

motioned them inside. "Make yourselves at home. If you're hungry, order something. I'll let him know that you're here."

Bailey had thought about that, and maybe Willow's presence was an answer, a way to solve this without confrontation. She reached into her purse and pulled out the envelope.

"I don't need to see him. Could you give this to him? And if he'd like to see Meg, we can arrange that."

Willows eyes softened and she smiled. "Bailey, he wants to see Meg. He would want to see you, too."

Why did Bailey's heart react to that information, as if it was what she'd wanted to hear but been afraid to ask? She didn't want to be a sixteen-year-old, asking if a boy missed her. She bit down on her bottom lip and shook her head to clear her thoughts. She couldn't do this again. She couldn't handle letting him walk away a third time.

She didn't want to be an expert at letting go. And she didn't want Meg to learn lessons about letting go. In life it happened, but it didn't have to be the only lesson. Shouldn't there be a lesson about hanging on and making something work?

Cody obviously didn't want to be that person in Bailey's life, the one who made it work. His letter made that as clear as an April morning. And thinking it through, allowing herself to think about how much she really wanted that, made her heart ache.

"I'll give him your message." Willow stepped forward and gave her a stiff hug. "It'll all work out."

Bailey watched her unexpected friend walk away. As the door closed softly behind Willow, Bailey thought about what the other woman had said about everything working out. Didn't all things work together for good for those who trusted God?

The television came on, the theme music of a children's

program breaking the silence of the room. Bailey smiled at Meg, who had curled up on the sofa with a box of cookies Willow had tossed her way. Willow didn't seem to know what to do with children.

With her daughter occupied, Bailey sat down in a chair next to the floor-to-ceiling window that looked out on the city of Las Vegas. Cody was out there somewhere, thinking he had worked everything out. He had rescued her, given her the land and made a promise to be a part of his daughter's life.

He didn't seem to have any trouble letting go.

Cody walked through the crowd toward the table that had been set up for autographs. People were staring, whispering; a crowd was forming. He didn't know what in the world was going on, but he sure wasn't comfortable with it.

"Big news." Jason had disappeared and reappeared now at his side, wearing one of his cheesiest smiles. Some people said he looked like England's Prince Harry. Cody preferred Opie, of *The Andy Griffith Show*.

"What's the big news? I'm going to win, but we all know that already."

Jason laughed and scooted out a folding chair to sit down. He pointed to the chair next to his for Cody.

"The big news is not you. The big news is the little girl who announced to everyone who would listen that you're her daddy. They say she had big blue eyes and dimples. Sound familiar?"

Cody jumped up, and the folding chair collapsed to the floor with a clang that drew more stares. Jason laughed and set the chair back up. He pointed for Cody to sit down.

"Calm down or you'll give it away. Look, here comes Willow and I think she's looking for you. She obviously isn't looking for me."

"She isn't looking for you because you welded her trailer gate closed."

"That was pretty funny."

"This isn't." Cody signed a poster that a little boy held out to him, and a hat that his dad held. "You all have a good day."

He smiled because that's what he was being paid for. His heart was chasing butterflies around his stomach. He rubbed a hand over his face and groaned.

"Cody, come with me."

"What?" He stared at Willow; she'd obviously gone crazy. He couldn't walk away right now.

She handed him an envelope and pushed Jason from his seat. Jason stood next to her, signing autographs and occasionally pushing something in front of Cody to sign.

Cody opened the envelope, knowing it was the one his lawyer had sent to Bailey. He read Bailey's note, that she didn't want his land and she wasn't letting him get away with walking out on Meg.

Walking out on Meg? He stood up, nearly knocking over the can of soda Jason had set on the table. "What does this mean?"

Willow shrugged. "I don't have the answer. I do have Bailey and Meg in my suite."

He looked across the room and made contact with one of the event organizers. Tad started and then shrugged. Cody stuffed the envelope into his pocket and followed Willow to the elevators.

"Why is she doing this?" he asked as the elevator doors closed them into the bronze-paneled box.

"She's protecting her heart." Willow pushed the top button.

Willow's pockets were deep, and Cody's respect for her had nothing to do with the dozen bulls she owned. He respected her because she was doing something for herself.

He pushed his hat down on his forehead and tried to regain some composure. He tried to find the answer he thought he'd already found, the one he'd been praying about.

When the door opened to the suite, Bailey looked up, surprise shining in her eyes. Meg ran across the room and threw herself into her dad's arms.

Bailey didn't.

"We've been looking for you," Meg warned in a whisper.

"I know. And I've been looking for you, too. For longer than I realized." He looked at Bailey as he said the words. "Do me a favor, Meg. Would you go with Willow and have ice cream so I can talk to your mom?"

"We'll go in the other room. I have fruit over there."

Meg nodded and slid to the ground. She looked from Cody to her mom and back to Cody again. Her little chin came up and she frowned. "I hope you two can be nice to each other."

Bailey covered her face with her hands. Cody thought she was crying. As the door closed behind Meg and Willow's departure, he realized she was laughing.

The laughter drew him to her, like a thirsty man to a well. She looked up, her eyes luminous in the dimly lit suite. Behind her the sky was a shimmering pink and the buildings were starting to light up.

It all dimmed in comparison with Bailey Cross and the way she made him feel, the way she'd always made him feel. What man in his right mind would run from a woman who completed him, who made him feel as if no matter what he was going through, if she was by his side, everything would be okay?

But what woman in her right mind would give a man like him a second chance to prove that she might possibly be everything to him?

He could start with two words and pray she gave him the opportunity to say the rest.

"Bailey, I'm sorry."

Bailey heard the words, but she couldn't get them straight in her mind, not yet. What exactly was Cody sorry for? And now that he was standing there in front of her, what was she going to do?

She'd spent the last two days memorizing what she'd say to him and how she'd set him straight. Now she could only stare at the cowboy in the red shirt and faded jeans, his white teeth flashing a hesitant smile in his suntanned face. She could think only about how right it felt when he was in her life and how wrong it felt when he walked away.

"So I guess we've been warned to play nice." His smile grew from hesitant to something that melted the ice.

"She learned that from her teacher. That's what Mrs. Parker says to Meg and her new friend Julie when they fight." Bailey explained.

He nodded, his jaw clenching and his gaze drifting from her to the window. He looked every inch a professional bull rider. And he looked like someone she wanted in her life.

He also looked a little bit upset. His blue eyes looked like a spring storm on the horizon. So much for the warm feelings that had erupted when he took that first step forward. Now she was feeling more like a person who had misunderstood.

"I didn't come to fight." Not really.

"I can play nice if you can." He tossed the envelope on the table. "What's this about?"

"You go first. You tell me why you sent it."

"Because I didn't want to take it from you. I never meant for you to think that."

"I know you didn't mean to take it. But sending it back felt a lot like goodbye. I can't let you do that to Meg." She picked up the envelope but kept her gaze connected with his. "Taking this would mean giving you permission to be a temporary visitor in Meg's life."

"What about you?" He had moved while they talked, and now he was right in front of her.

He stood near enough to touch—if she had wanted to touch him. She could even walk into his arms and be held. She didn't want that. She was here because of Meg.

"I can let you go." She didn't want to. She no longer wanted to be good at letting go. She hadn't had a choice with her dad. She hadn't had a choice the first time Cody left.

"What if…?" He leaned close, his aftershave as cool as a spring morning. "What if I don't want to let you go?"

He leaned, his lips barely grazing hers, and then he took a step back. Bailey wasn't able to disengage so easily. Her breath was trapped painfully in her chest, and she wanted to step into his arms forever.

With eyes closed, she counted to ten, hoping she'd open them to find herself in control of the situation and her emotions. While she counted, her mind registered his words. She'd been so determined to set him straight that she hadn't really paid attention because she hadn't wanted to argue.

She opened her eyes, blinking to clear her vision. What she saw was Cody in front of her, looking as if he was waiting for an answer.

"Weren't we talking about you giving back the land, the only tie that you had to us?"

"We were talking about that, but I think we both know that the land isn't what ties me to Gibson, Missouri."

"Meg will always be there, and you'll always be in her life."

"And you?"

"What about me?"

"I don't want to be the person you regret."

Bailey covered her face with her hands, thinking of that day in the diner and the bell that had clanked over the door.

"You heard me say that?"

"I did. And I took it to heart."

Bailey rested her hand on his cheek and his eyes closed. "Cody, the only thing I regret is that you only wanted to marry me to give Meg a family. I regret mistakes I've made. I regret that I can't seem to let go of you."

"Why are you so determined to let go?"

"Because you're so determined to leave."

"I proposed."

She shook her head and walked away. Staring out over the city skyline, she tried to figure out where the conversation was going and why it wasn't going the way she had rehearsed.

"You proposed to solve a problem."

From behind he reached for her hands and tucked his head close to hers, Bailey closed her eyes at his nearness and the feeling that this was right and that it should be forever. She tried to remember why it couldn't be.

"I wanted to marry you because I love you," he whispered, and then he brushed a soft kiss across her cheek. "I want forever. I just didn't realize it until it was too late."

"Is it too late?"

Bailey clasped his hands in hers and leaned back into his embrace. He turned her to face him. As he stared down at her, she waited with breath held and a heart full of hope. It seemed as if they were both good at racing off to say one thing and then finding out there was another plan.

"I don't think it's too late. I think it's just in time," he whispered. "Let me try this again, Bailey."

He held her hands and drew her close. "Marry me, because I love you and I want to be more than a father to Meg. I want to be your husband, the man you can count on."

A squeal interrupted the moment, and Bailey had to admit it had been a moment. Her legs were Jell-O and her heart was still trying to catch up with everything Cody had said. She hadn't even answered yet, because Meg was suddenly there and in his arms. And they looked like a family.

Willow stood at the door, her cheeks flushed. "Sorry, she escaped."

Meg leaned to whisper in Cody's ear. "We were listening at the door."

"Gotta run now. You all take your time in here." Willow said from the door. "Cody, I'll let them know you're on your way down."

"Well?" Meg was in Cody's arms, and they were both looking at Bailey, matching blue eyes and matching looks of determination.

"I'll think about it." She laughed and they didn't. "I thought about it."

"And?" Cody stepped close again, Meg's arms around his neck. She was obviously outnumbered.

"And I love you and I want forever with you."

"Forever won't be long enough."

"I wonder if they have a reservation at the Elvis Chapel?"

"Because when in Vegas…" Cody shook his head. "Sorry, honey, we're getting married in Gibson. After a nice long engagement of at least a month."

"A Christmas wedding?" Bailey closed her eyes, imagining the wedding and forever.

"Christmas is perfect." He hugged her again, a group hug

with Meg in the middle. "And now I have to go win the world title. Because this is my last year to ride bulls."

She liked the sound of that, because it meant not letting go again.

* * * * *

Want more heart-stopping cowboys?
Check out A COWBOY'S HEART from Brenda Minton
in February 2009, only from Love Inspired!

Dear Reader,

I hope that you enjoyed reading Cody and Bailey's story, and I hope that you loved Meg, with her yellow sundress and pink boots. It is my deepest wish that reading this book took you on a journey, tugged your emotions and gave you something to think about when you reached THE END.

How did this book come about? The characters started it all. They came to me one day, popping into my head as if they were meant to be. From the moment their story started to pour out on paper, it was obvious they had something special to teach us about forgiving others, forgiving ourselves, and letting go—while holding on. It can all be summed up in Bailey's motto: Pull yourself up by the bootstraps and move on.

These characters were difficult for me to walk away from and I hope that you'll find yourself occasionally revisiting them, and Gibson, Missouri.

I love to hear from my readers. Please visit my Web site: www.brendaminton.net and drop me an e-mail.

Blessings,

Brenda Minton

QUESTIONS FOR DISCUSSION

1. Cody Jacobs arrives in Gibson, Missouri, because he's on step 9 of a 12-step program. He's making amends for past actions, and seeking the forgiveness of people he had hurt. We've all made mistakes, done things we're ashamed of, or hurt people we care about. How important is it to make amends with those that we've hurt?

2. Bailey has her own secret—the child that she and Cody share. At first, keeping this secret from him seemed like the best option. Now she sees her mistake. Time and distance make it more difficult to go back and undo mistakes and wrong decisions. What are some repercussions of avoiding rather than dealing with a situation?

3. Cody struggles with alcoholism. He is now sober and he wants to stay that way. He's learning to acknowledge when he feels weak, and to withstand temptation. We all struggle with some type of temptation. What does the Bible say about temptation, and how to deal with it?

4. Bailey had to put aside self. Her first reaction is to push Cody from her life. But there are other people to think about. Her daughter, her father and Cody. How can considering the needs of others help us to put our own wants into perspective?

5. Bailey wants to do everything on her own. There is a thin line between being strong and being prideful. We all need help at some time in our lives. What does the Bible say about pride and humility?

6. When Bailey came home pregnant she found it hard to face the people in her community and her church. She felt judged. And she also judged herself for her mistake. What reaches a person: judging, pointing out their sin, or showing the love of Christ and forgiveness? For all have sinned and fallen short of the glory of God.

7. What could have happened to Bailey if there hadn't been people willing to love her and help her through her pregnancy? Is there someone in your life, your church or community that could use a word of encouragement or the reassurance that mistakes happen and can be overcome?

8. Bailey, like so many of us, was looking for answers and a way to get through a difficult time. She faced the loss of her father, the possibility of losing her farm and then the arrival of her daughter's father. There were moments when she went into self-preservation mode, looking for answers, but not really looking to God. And God did have a plan. It is easy to try and "fix" problems in our lives. How are situations changed when we seek God and His will?

9. If we believe that God has a purpose for our lives, shouldn't we also believe that He has a plan, a direct way for bringing about that purpose? In Bailey's life, Cody was a part of God's plan.

10. People in Gibson, Missouri, were only too glad to have a little something extra to gossip about. Cody's presence at Bailey's provided the sourse of gossip. Some "sins" are obvious. We all know it is wrong to lie, to steal, to kill. Other sins, like gossip, are comfortable sins that fly

around under the radar. Can a little "gossip" ever really be harmless?

11. Bailey's father left footprints of faith for his daughter and granddaughter. We all leave footprints as we walk through life. Have you examined your own footprints, the legacy you are leaving behind? Are there things you could change now that might make a difference in the lives of those who look up to you?

12. Cody sometimes doubted his ability to be the person he needed to be for Meg. But he made right choices—one decision at a time. He stayed in his daughter's life. He turned away from the temptation to drink. He gave Bailey space. We make one decision at a time, praying for the best. What steps do we take if we, or someone we're counting on, makes a wrong choice?

13. Communication 101: don't let misunderstanding remain between you and the people you love. Talk it out. Years ago Cody ignored Bailey's phone calls. Now Bailey misunderstands the land that Cody bought and gave to her. When we walk away from a misunderstanding without resolving it, we walk away from something that might have been fixed with just a few words of explanation. Are there situations in your own life that could be fixed with a conversation and forgiveness?

REQUEST YOUR FREE BOOKS!

2 FREE INSPIRATIONAL NOVELS
PLUS 2
FREE
MYSTERY GIFTS

Love Inspired®

YES! Please send me 2 FREE Love Inspired® novels and my 2 FREE mystery gifts (gifts are worth about $10). After receiving them, if I don't wish to receive any more books, I can return the shipping statement marked "cancel". If I don't cancel, I will receive 4 brand-new novels every month and be billed just $4.24 per book in the U.S. or $4.74 per book in Canada, plus 25¢ shipping and handling per book and applicable taxes, if any*. That's a savings of over 20% off the cover price! I understand that accepting the 2 free books and gifts places me under no obligation to buy anything. I can always return a shipment and cancel at any time. Even if I never buy another book, the two free books and gifts are mine to keep forever.

113 IDN ERXA   313 IDN ERWX

Name	(PLEASE PRINT)	
Address		Apt. #
City	State/Prov.	Zip/Postal Code

Signature (if under 18, a parent or guardian must sign)

Order online at www.LoveInspiredBooks.com

Or mail to Steeple Hill Reader Service:

IN U.S.A.: P.O. Box 1867, Buffalo, NY 14240-1867
IN CANADA: P.O. Box 609, Fort Erie, Ontario L2A 5X3

Not valid to current subscribers of Love Inspired books.

Want to try two free books from another series?
Call 1-800-873-8635 or visit www.morefreebooks.com

* Terms and prices subject to change without notice. N.Y. residents add applicable sales tax. Canadian residents will be charged applicable provincial taxes and GST. Offer not valid in Quebec. This offer is limited to one order per household. All orders subject to approval. Credit or debit balances in a customer's account(s) may be offset by any other outstanding balance owed by or to the customer. Please allow 4 to 6 weeks for delivery. Offer available while quantities last.

Your Privacy: Steeple Hill Books is committed to protecting your privacy. Our Privacy Policy is available online at www.SteepleHill.com or upon request from the Reader Service. From time to time we make our lists of customers available to reputable third parties who may have a product or service of interest to you. If you would prefer we not share your name and address, please check here. ☐

LIREG08R

TITLES AVAILABLE NEXT MONTH

Don't miss these four stories in November

FROM THIS DAY FORWARD by Irene Hannon
Heartland Homecomings

After a frightening attack, Cara Martin needed a safe haven. So she accepted her estranged husband's offer to share his home. The man who'd broken her heart had become a different person—no longer a workaholic surgeon but now a general doc who cared about people. Could their relationship be healed?

GIVING THANKS FOR BABY by Terri Reed
A Tiny Blessings Tale

Trista Van Zant came to Chestnut Grove to start over with her infant son. Still healing from a painful divorce, she found comfort with local pastor Scott Crosby. But when her ex came to town demanding custody, could Trista see beyond her present trials to trust God for her future?

SHEPHERDS ABIDING IN DRY CREEK by Janet Tronstad
Dry Creek

Dry Creek, Montana, looked like the perfect place for Marla Gossett to raise her children. But an unusual theft cast suspicion on her family and brought deputy sheriff Les Wilkerson into her life. Now she'd have to depend on this big-hearted lawman to save her family.

YULETIDE HOMECOMING by Carolyne Aarsen

Sarah Westerveld's father summoned her home after years of estrangement, but a stroke delayed their long-awaited talk. Sarah desired to be forgiven for the past. Yet that past—and the future she dreamed of—included darkly handsome Logan Carleton, son of her father's sworn enemy.